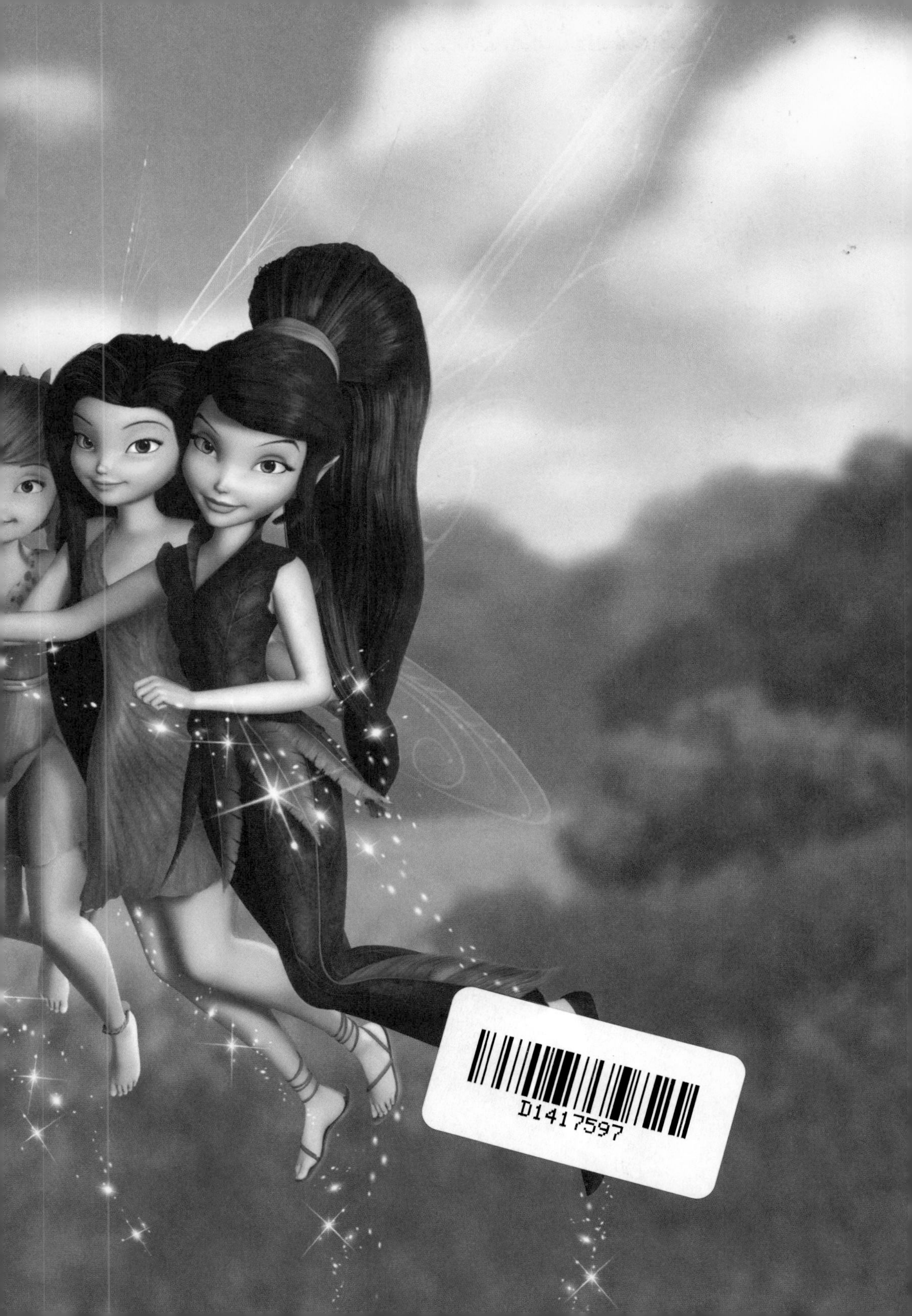

TinkerBell
AND THE
GREAT FAIRY RESCUE

The Graphic Novel

PAPERCUTZ

Disney fairies

Graphic Novels Available from
PAPERCUTZ

Graphic Novel #1
"Prilla's Talent"

Graphic Novel #2
"Tinker Bell and
the Wings of Rani"

COMING SOON:

Graphic Novel #3
"Tinker Bell and the
Day of the Dragon"

Graphic Novel #4
"Tinker Bell
to the Rescue"

Graphic Novel #5
"Tinker Bell and the
Pirate Adventure"

Discover fairy games
and activities at:
www.disneyfairies.com

TinkerBell
GREAT FAIRY RESCUE

is available on

MAGIC IN HIGH DEFINITION

"Tinker Bell and the Great Fairy Rescue"
Created by Global Magazines Editorial Team
Disney Publishing Worldwide
Bianca Coletti: Editorial Director
Roberto Santillo: Creative Director
Guido Frazzini: Director, Franchise
Editorial Development

Script: Augusto Machetto
Revised Captions: Stefan Petrucha
Layout: Monica Catalano
Pencils: Davide Baldoni, Emilio Grasso, Sara S
Inks: Roberta Zanotta
Color: Studio Kawaii
Color Supervision: Stefano Attardi
Lettering: Janice Chiang
Cover: Walt Disney Studios Home Entertain
and DisneyToon Studios
Special Thanks to the DisneyToon Studios t

Project Design and Editing: If Edizioni - M

Papercutz Edition
Caitlin Hinrichs – Production
Michael Petranek – Editorial Assistant
Jim Salicrup – Editor-in-Chief

ISBN: 978-1-59707-232-8
Copyright © 2010 by Disney Enterprises, I
All rights reserved.

Printed in Canada
July 2010 by Friesens
1 Printer's Way
Altona, MB R0G 0B0

Distributed by Macmillan.
First Printing

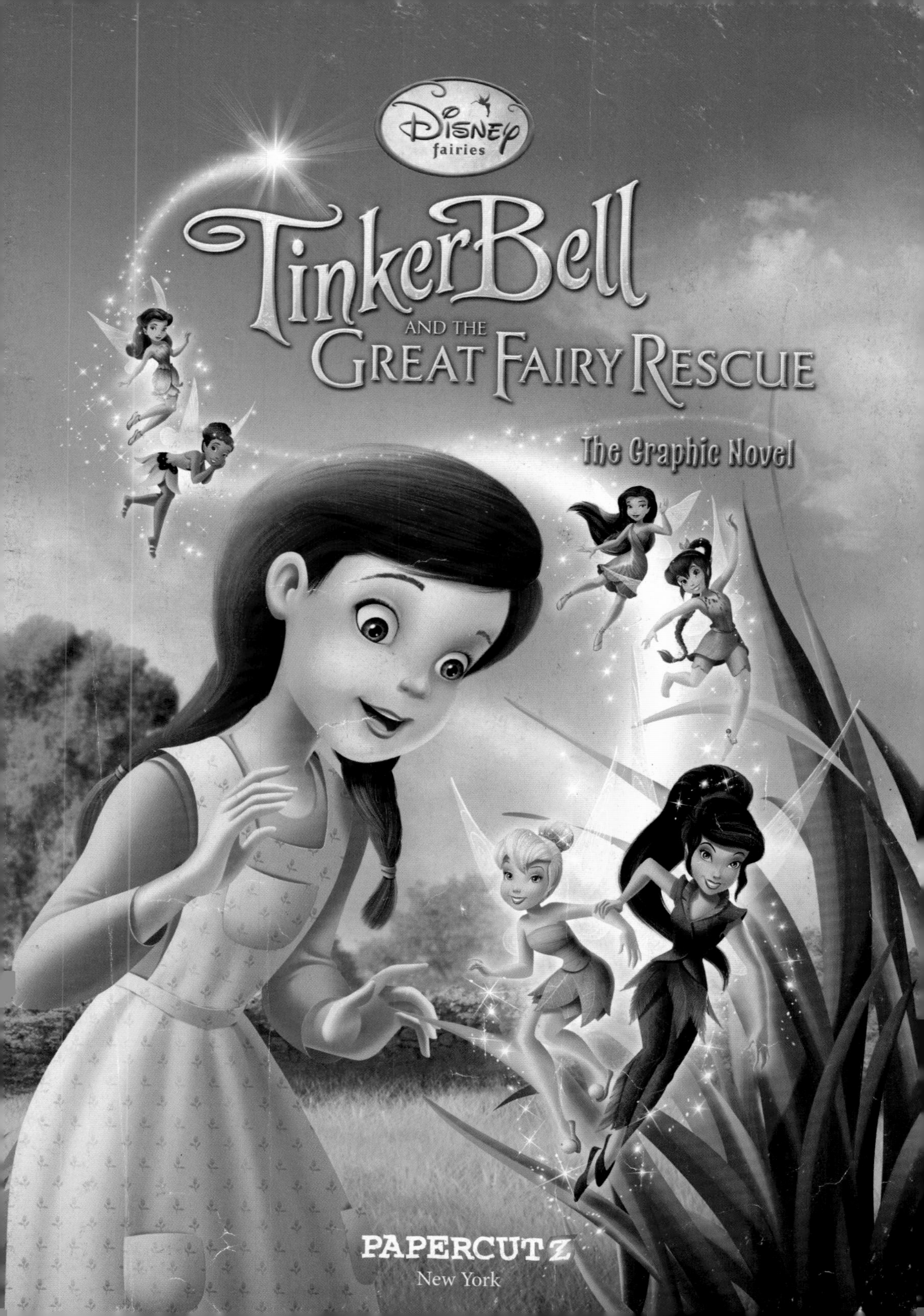
Disney fairies
Tinker Bell
and the
Great Fairy Rescue
The Graphic Novel
PAPERCUTZ
New York

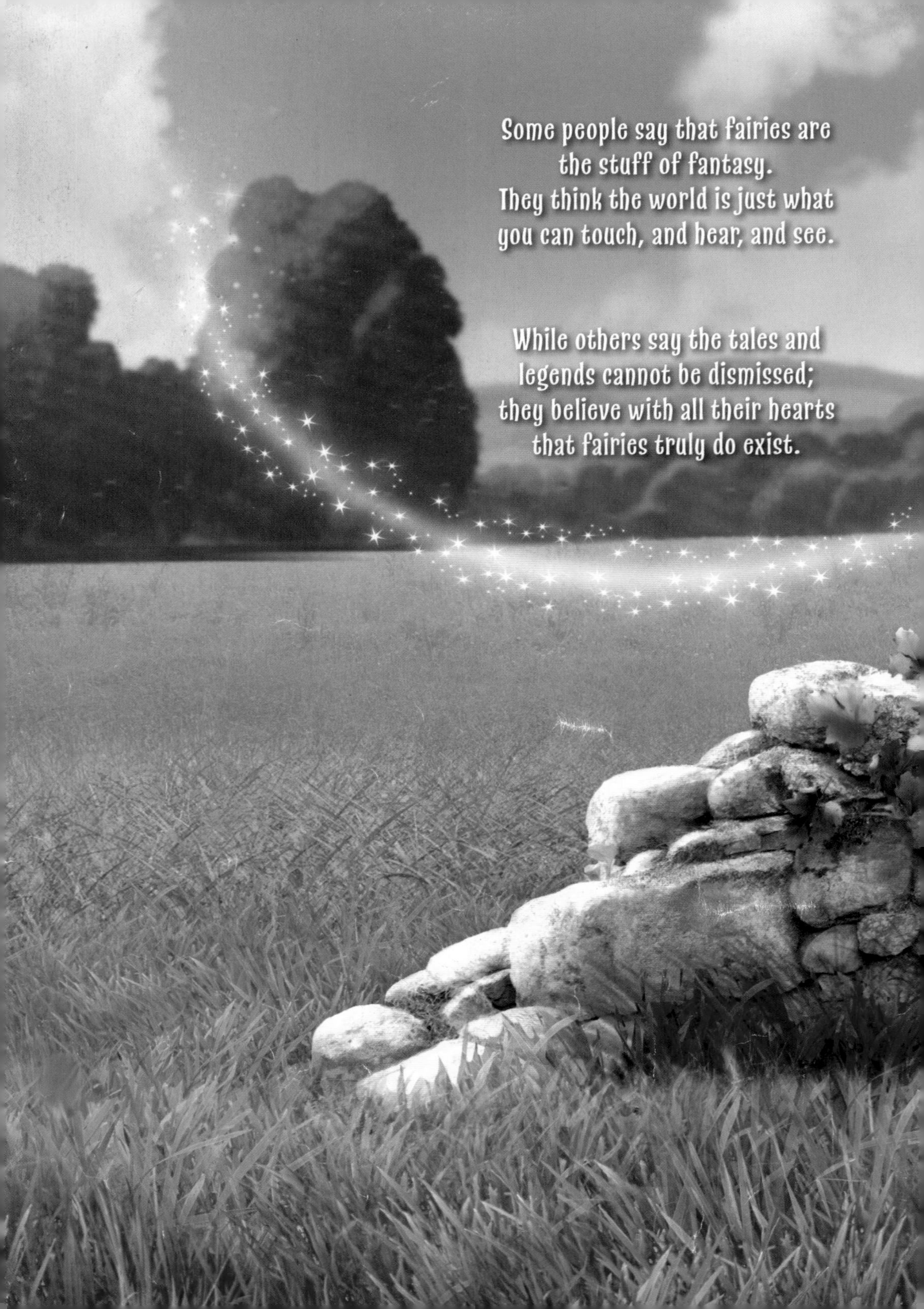

Some people say that fairies are
the stuff of fantasy.
They think the world is just what
you can touch, and hear, and see.

While others say the tales and
legends cannot be dismissed;
they believe with all their hearts
that fairies truly do exist.

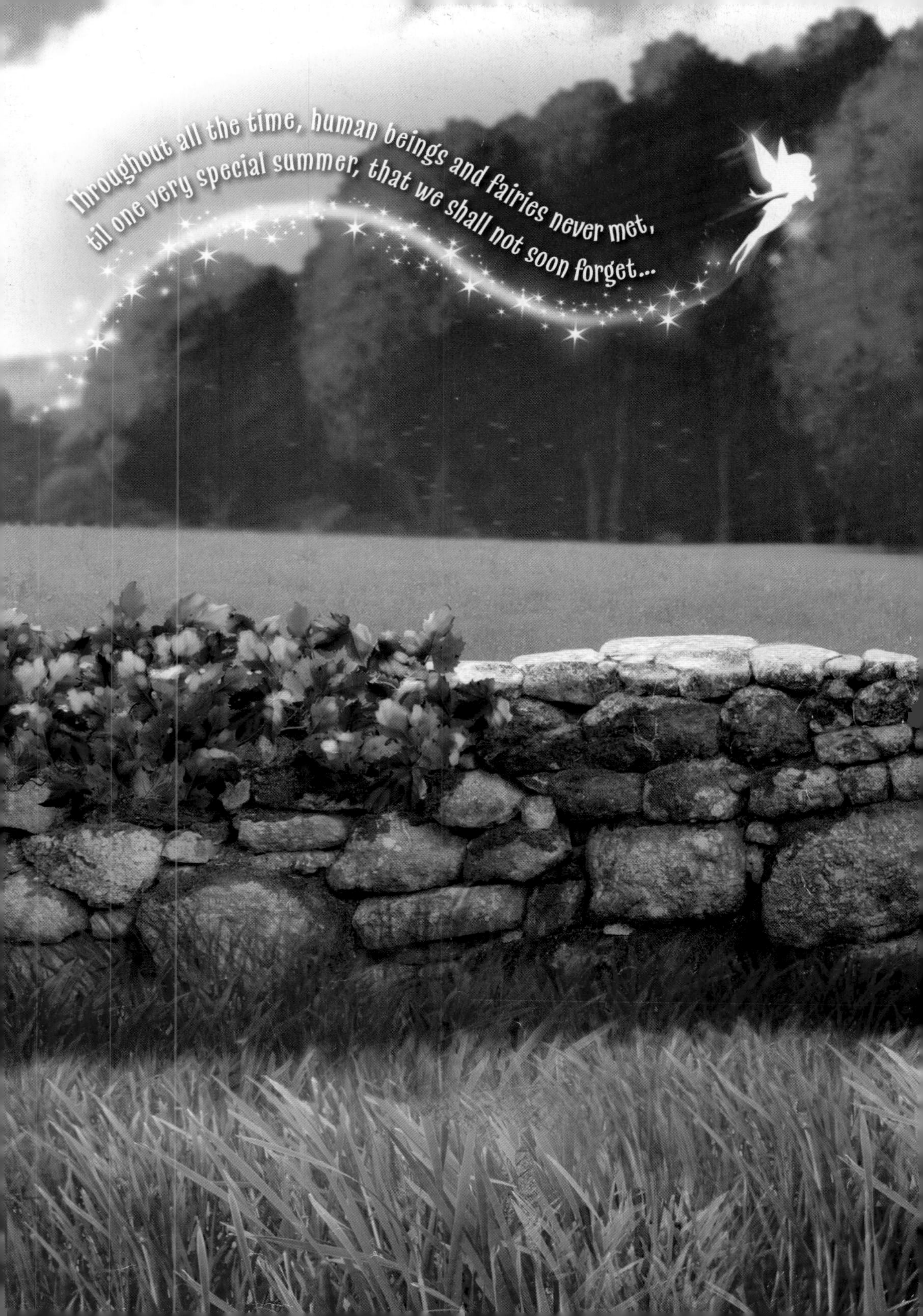
Throughout all the time, human beings and fairies never met,
til one very special summer, that we shall not soon forget...

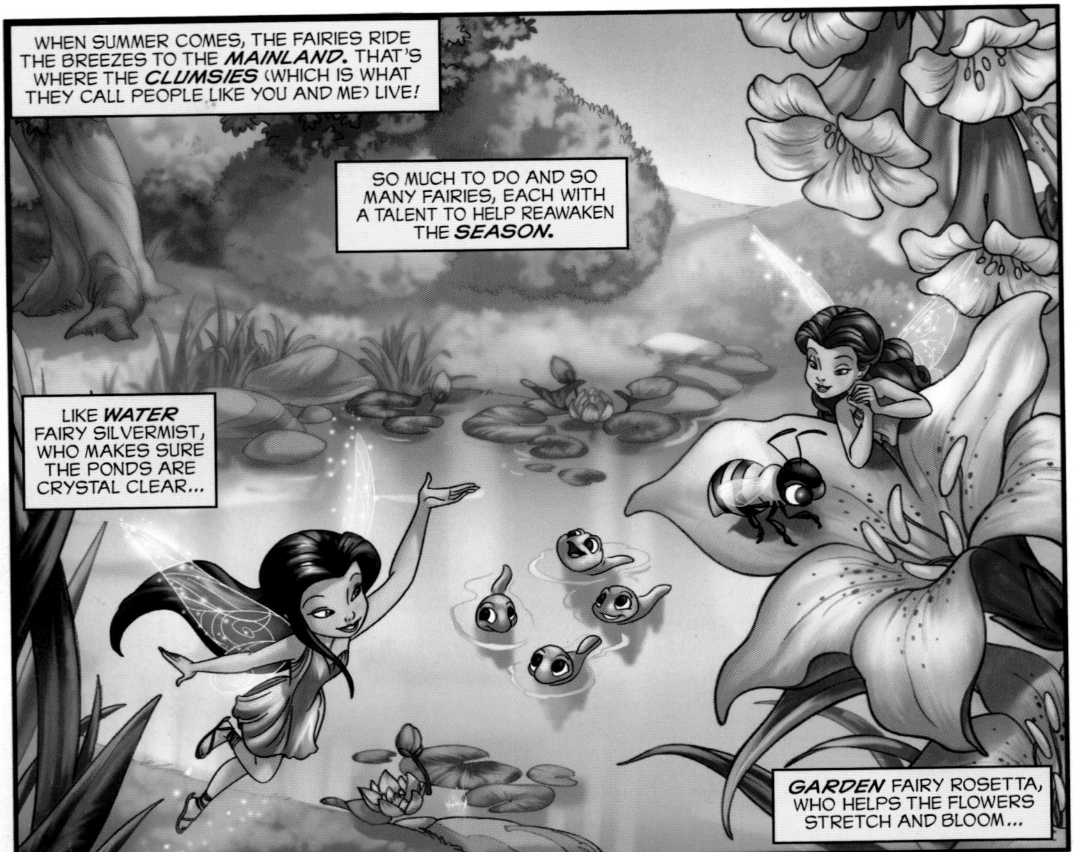
WHEN SUMMER COMES, THE FAIRIES RIDE THE BREEZES TO THE MAINLAND. THAT'S WHERE THE CLUMSIES (WHICH IS WHAT THEY CALL PEOPLE LIKE YOU AND ME) LIVE!
SO MUCH TO DO AND SO MANY FAIRIES, EACH WITH A TALENT TO HELP REAWAKEN THE SEASON.
LIKE WATER FAIRY SILVERMIST, WHO MAKES SURE THE PONDS ARE CRYSTAL CLEAR...
GARDEN FAIRY ROSETTA, WHO HELPS THE FLOWERS STRETCH AND BLOOM...

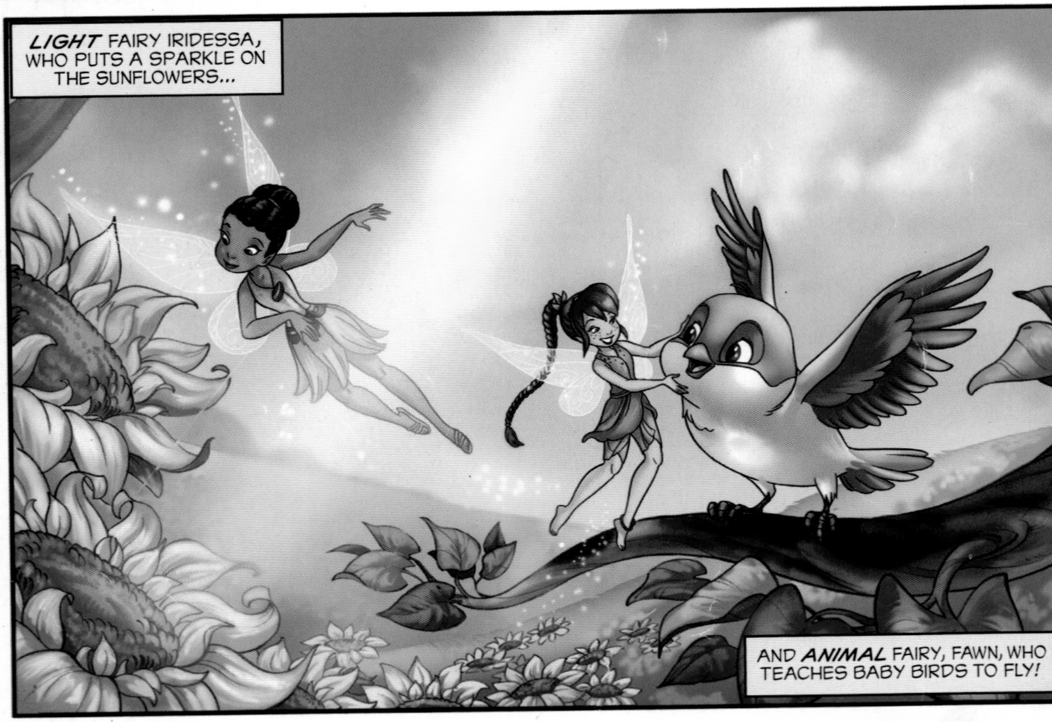
LIGHT FAIRY IRIDESSA, WHO PUTS A SPARKLE ON THE SUNFLOWERS...
AND ANIMAL FAIRY, FAWN, WHO TEACHES BABY BIRDS TO FLY!

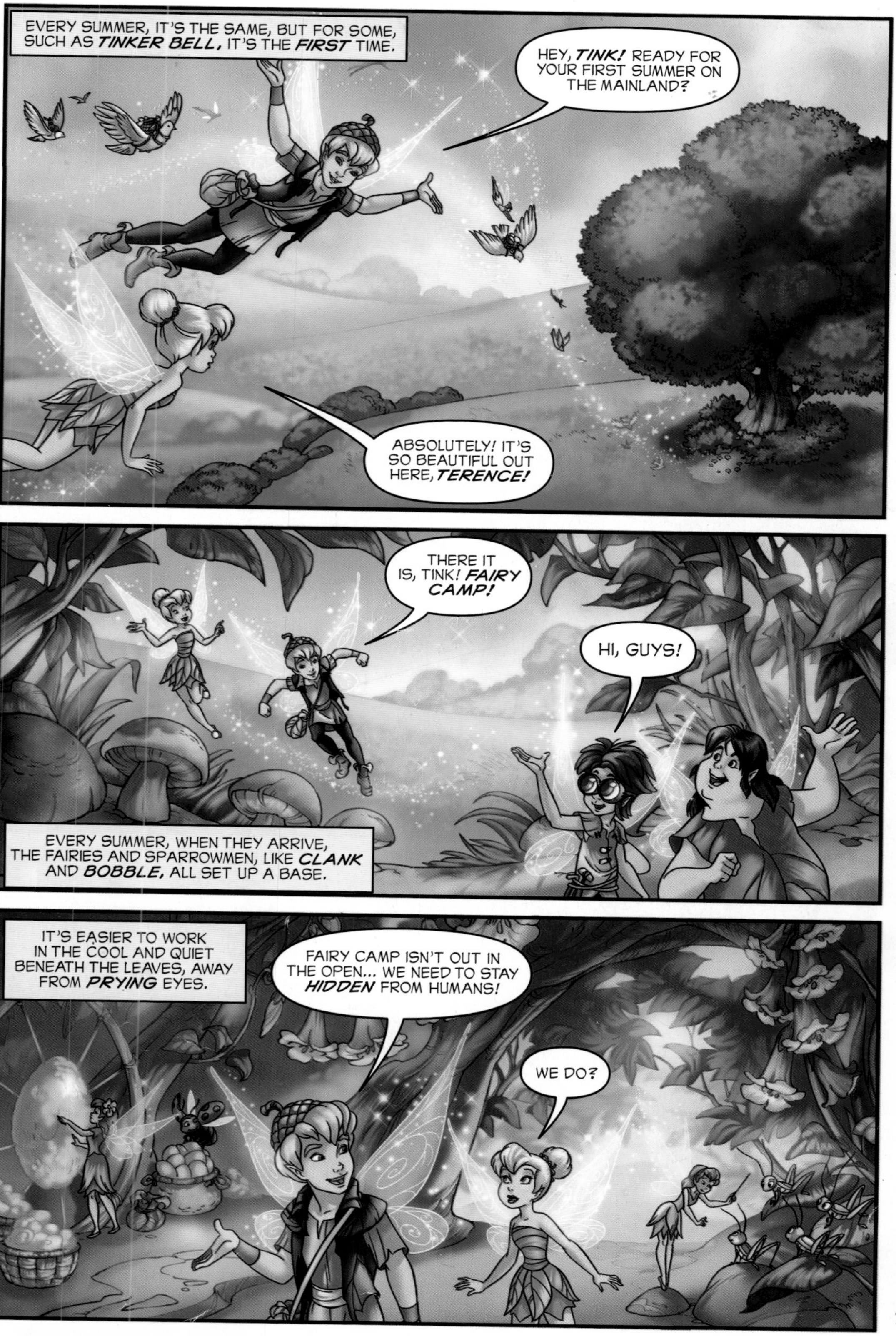
EVERY SUMMER, IT'S THE SAME, BUT FOR SOME, SUCH AS TINKER BELL, IT'S THE FIRST TIME.
HEY, TINK! READY FOR YOUR FIRST SUMMER ON THE MAINLAND?
ABSOLUTELY! IT'S SO BEAUTIFUL OUT HERE, TERENCE!
THERE IT IS, TINK! FAIRY CAMP!
HI, GUYS!
EVERY SUMMER, WHEN THEY ARRIVE, THE FAIRIES AND SPARROWMEN, LIKE CLANK AND BOBBLE, ALL SET UP A BASE.
IT'S EASIER TO WORK IN THE COOL AND QUIET BENEATH THE LEAVES, AWAY FROM PRYING EYES.
FAIRY CAMP ISN'T OUT IN THE OPEN... WE NEED TO STAY HIDDEN FROM HUMANS!
WE DO?

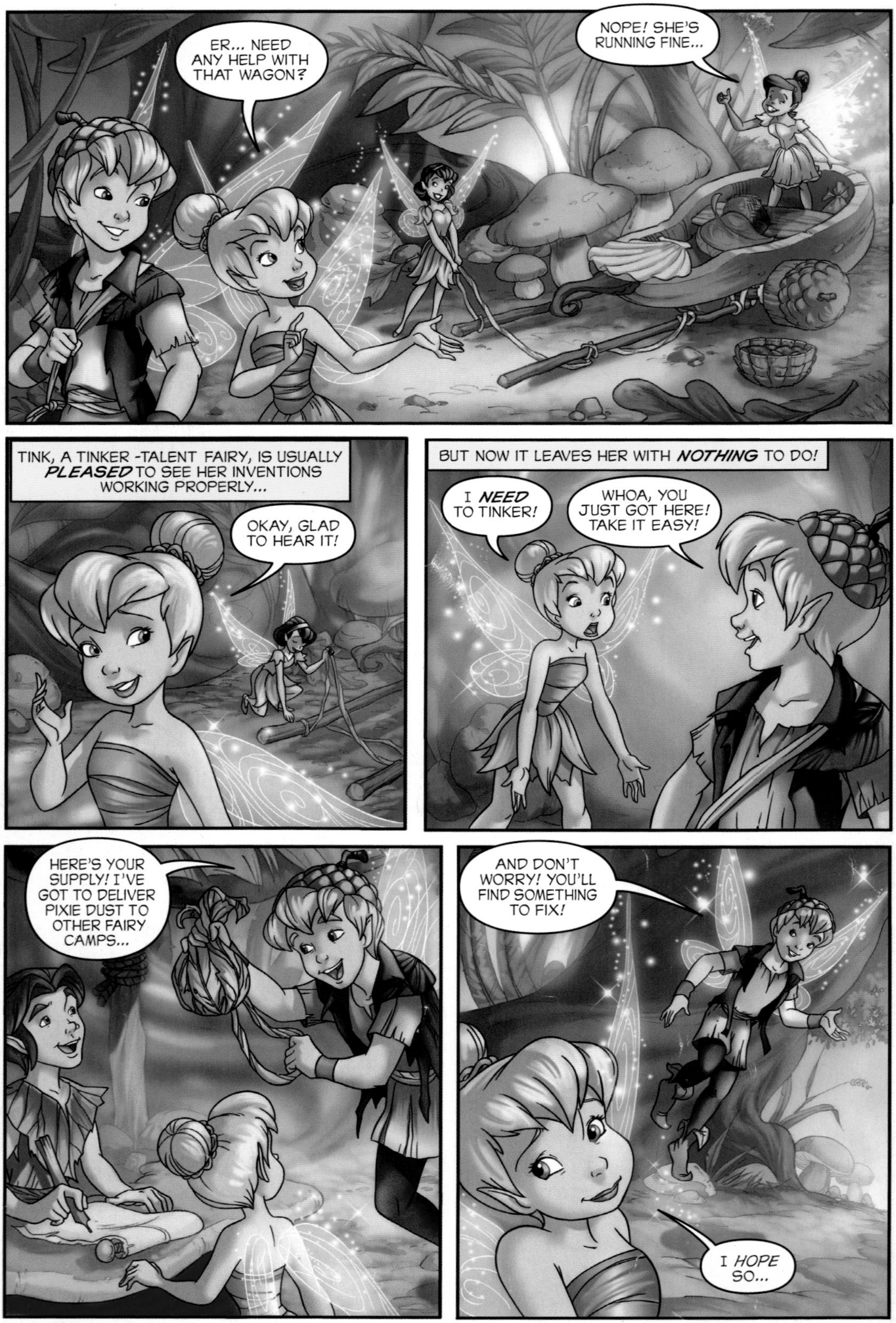
ER... NEED ANY HELP WITH THAT WAGON?
NOPE! SHE'S RUNNING FINE...
TINK, A TINKER -TALENT FAIRY, IS USUALLY *PLEASED* TO SEE HER INVENTIONS WORKING PROPERLY...
OKAY, GLAD TO HEAR IT!
BUT NOW IT LEAVES HER WITH *NOTHING* TO DO!
I *NEED* TO TINKER!
WHOA, YOU JUST GOT HERE! TAKE IT EASY!
HERE'S YOUR SUPPLY! I'VE GOT TO DELIVER PIXIE DUST TO OTHER FAIRY CAMPS...
AND DON'T WORRY! YOU'LL FIND SOMETHING TO FIX!
I *HOPE* SO...

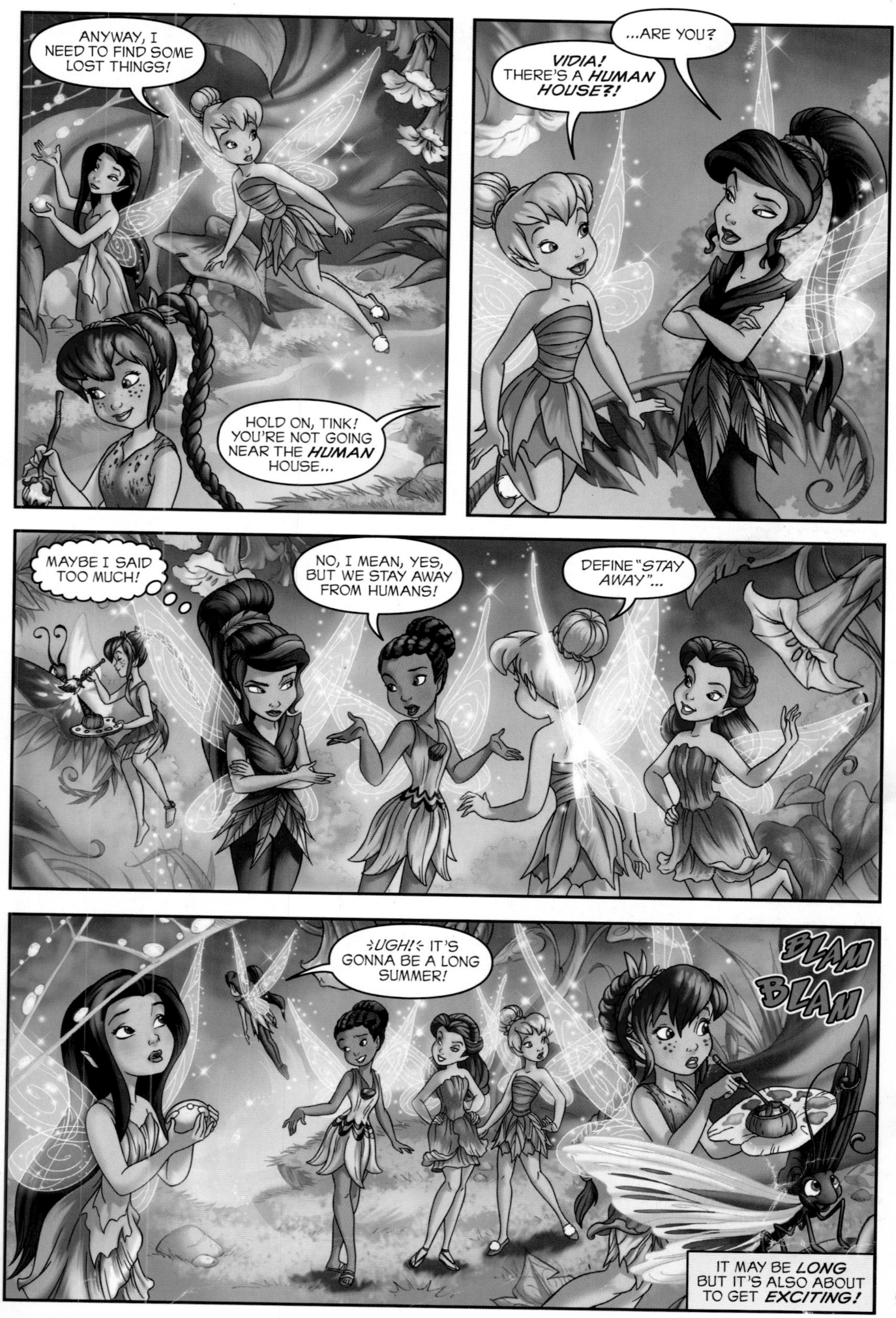
ANYWAY, I NEED TO FIND SOME LOST THINGS!
HOLD ON, TINK! YOU'RE NOT GOING NEAR THE *HUMAN* HOUSE...
VIDIA! THERE'S A *HUMAN HOUSE?!*
...ARE YOU?
MAYBE I SAID TOO MUCH!
NO, I MEAN, YES, BUT WE STAY AWAY FROM HUMANS!
DEFINE "*STAY AWAY*"...
UGH! IT'S GONNA BE A LONG SUMMER!
BLAM
BLAM
IT MAY BE *LONG* BUT IT'S ALSO ABOUT TO GET *EXCITING!*

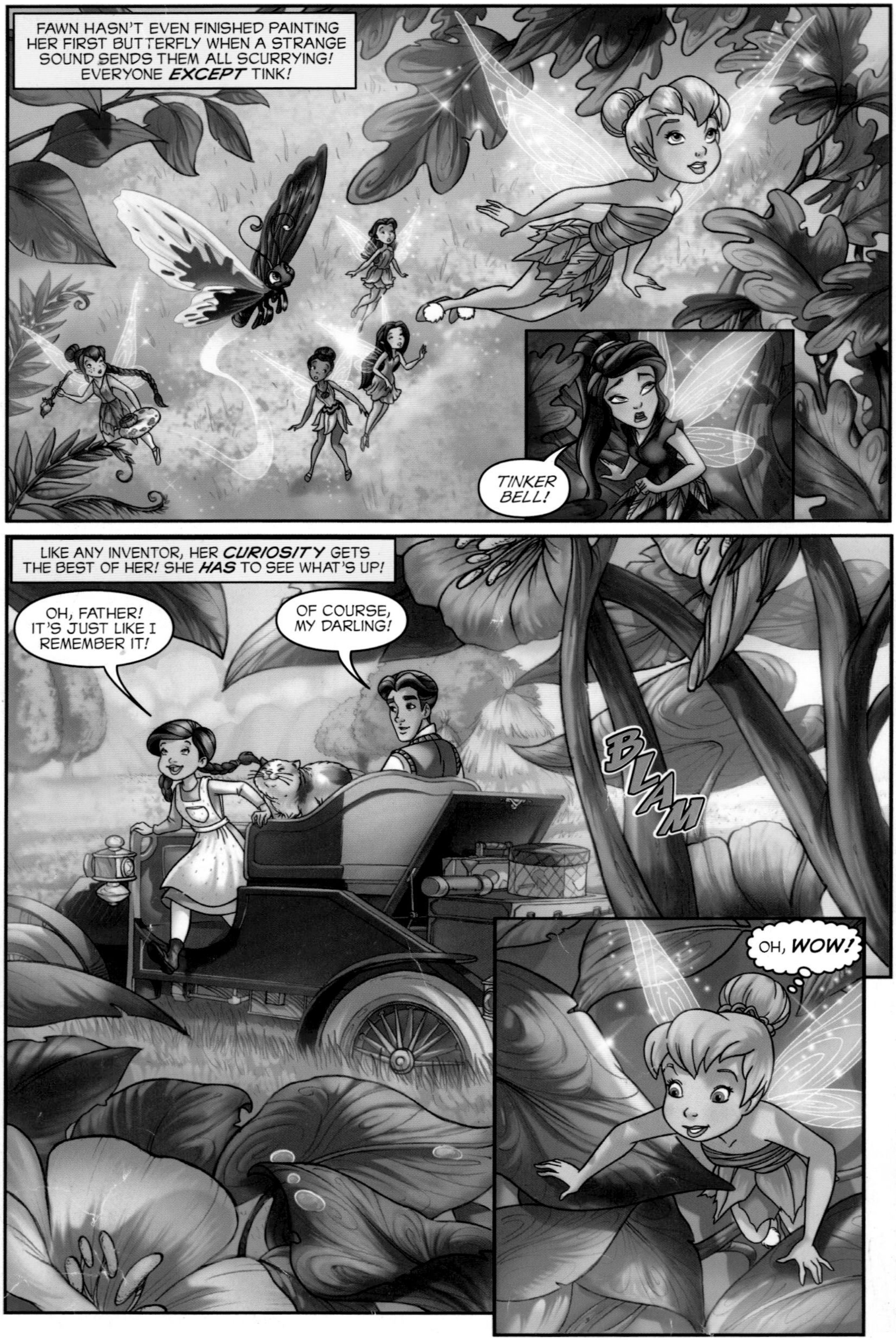
FAWN HASN'T EVEN FINISHED PAINTING HER FIRST BUTTERFLY WHEN A STRANGE SOUND SENDS THEM ALL SCURRYING! EVERYONE EXCEPT TINK!
TINKER BELL!
LIKE ANY INVENTOR, HER CURIOSITY GETS THE BEST OF HER! SHE HAS TO SEE WHAT'S UP!
OH, FATHER! IT'S JUST LIKE I REMEMBER IT!
OF COURSE, MY DARLING!
BLAM
OH, WOW!

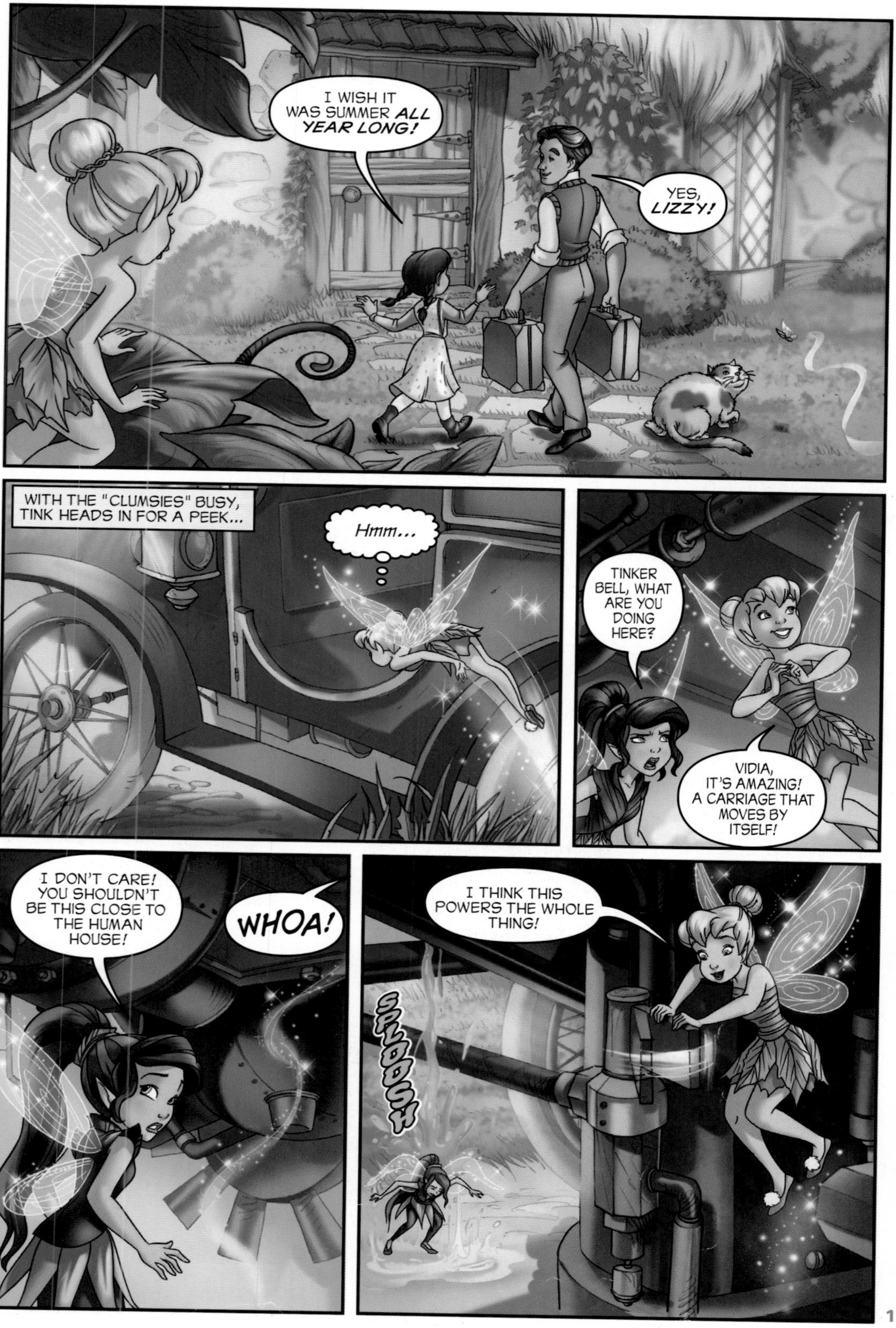

I WISH IT WAS SUMMER ALL YEAR LONG!
YES, LIZZY!
WITH THE "CLUMSIES" BUSY, TINK HEADS IN FOR A PEEK...
Hmm...
TINKER BELL, WHAT ARE YOU DOING HERE?
VIDIA, IT'S AMAZING! A CARRIAGE THAT MOVES BY ITSELF!
I DON'T CARE! YOU SHOULDN'T BE THIS CLOSE TO THE HUMAN HOUSE!
WHOA!
I THINK THIS POWERS THE WHOLE THING!
SPLOOSH

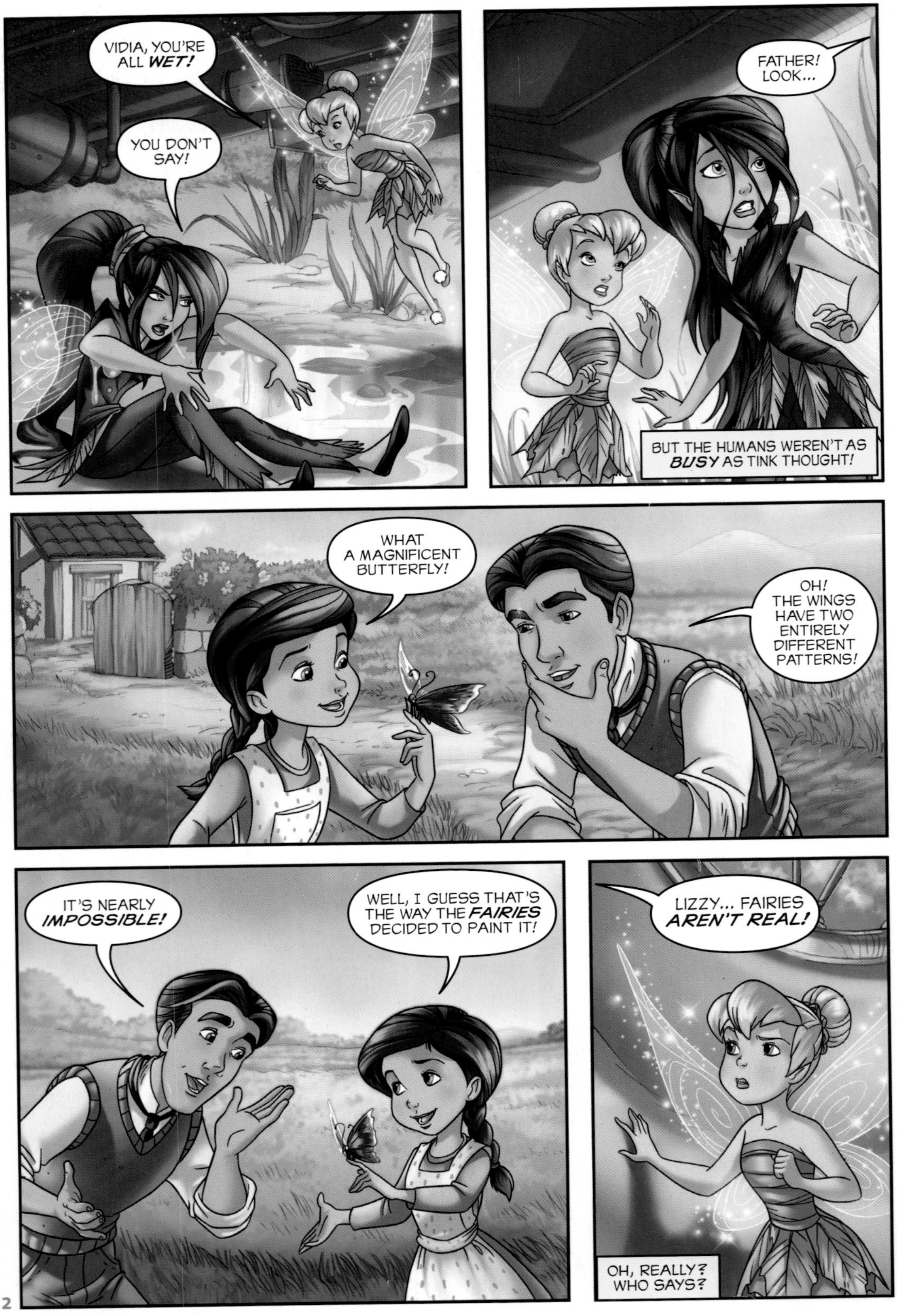
VIDIA, YOU'RE ALL **WET!**
YOU DON'T SAY!
FATHER! LOOK...
BUT THE HUMANS WEREN'T AS **BUSY** AS TINK THOUGHT!
WHAT A MAGNIFICENT BUTTERFLY!
OH! THE WINGS HAVE TWO ENTIRELY DIFFERENT PATTERNS!
IT'S NEARLY **IMPOSSIBLE!**
WELL, I GUESS THAT'S THE WAY THE **FAIRIES** DECIDED TO PAINT IT!
LIZZY... FAIRIES **AREN'T REAL!**
OH, REALLY? WHO SAYS?

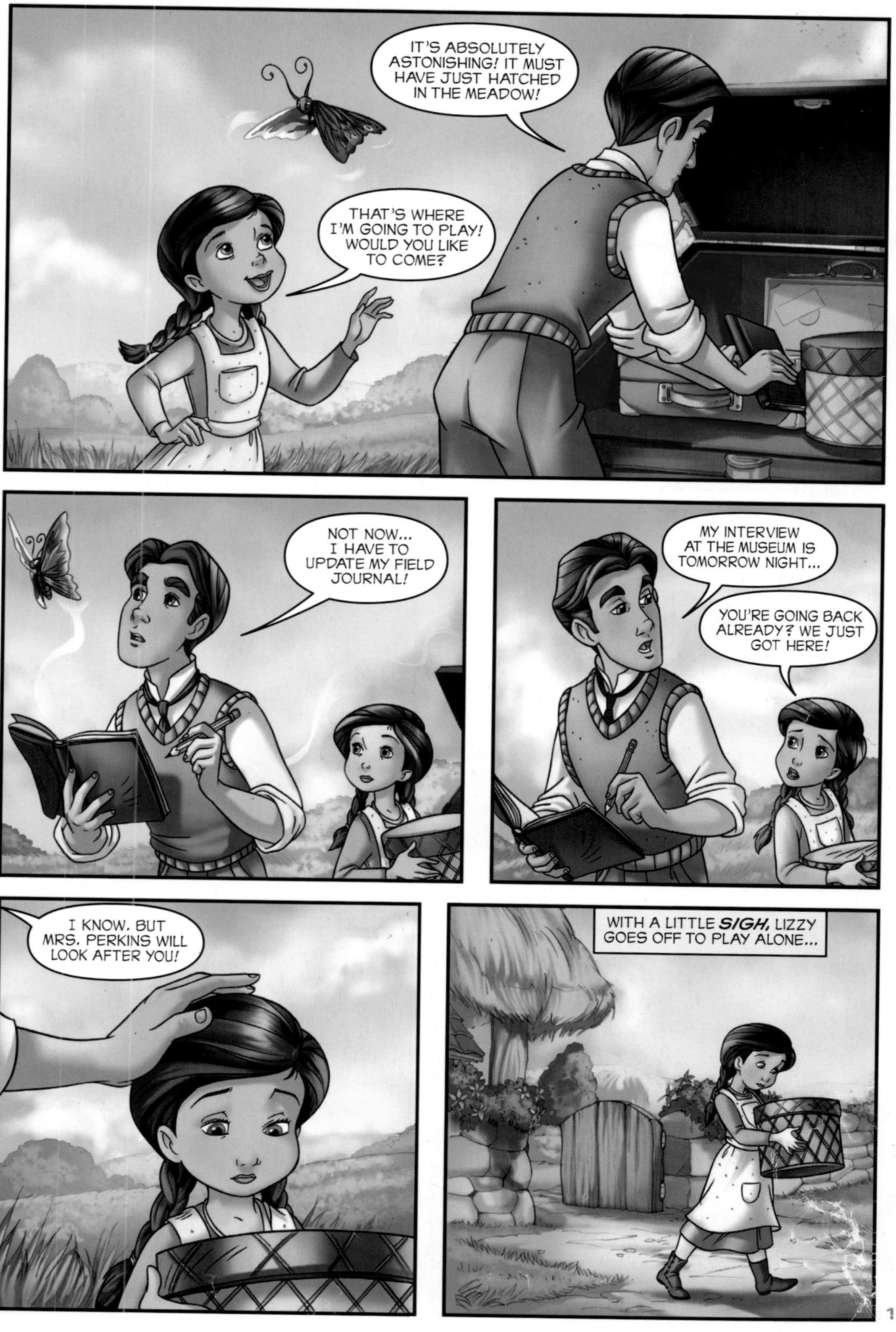
IT'S ABSOLUTELY ASTONISHING! IT MUST HAVE JUST HATCHED IN THE MEADOW!
THAT'S WHERE I'M GOING TO PLAY! WOULD YOU LIKE TO COME?
NOT NOW... I HAVE TO UPDATE MY FIELD JOURNAL!
MY INTERVIEW AT THE MUSEUM IS TOMORROW NIGHT...
YOU'RE GOING BACK ALREADY? WE JUST GOT HERE!
I KNOW. BUT MRS. PERKINS WILL LOOK AFTER YOU!
WITH A LITTLE SIGH, LIZZY GOES OFF TO PLAY ALONE...

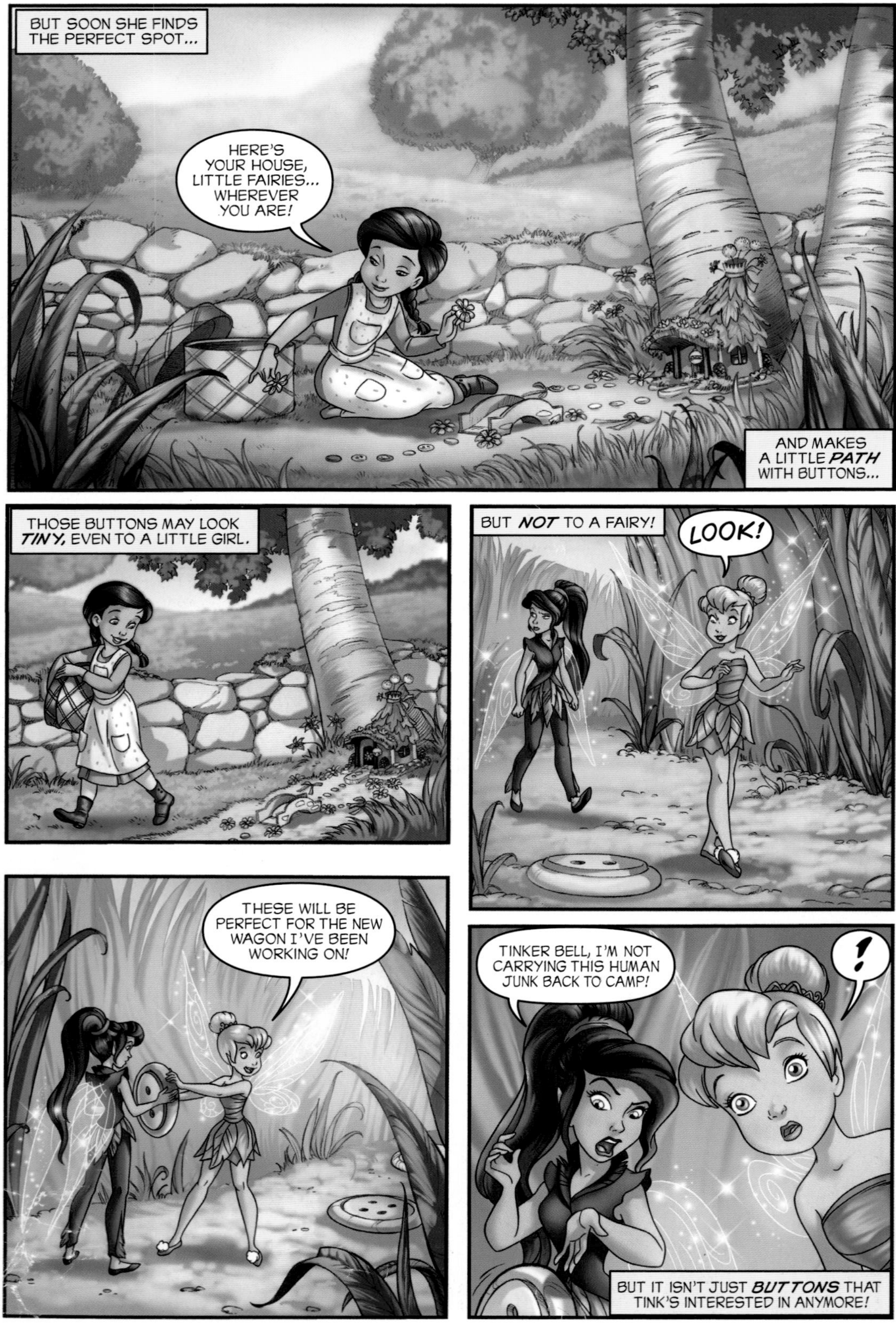
BUT SOON SHE FINDS THE PERFECT SPOT...
HERE'S YOUR HOUSE, LITTLE FAIRIES... WHEREVER YOU ARE!
AND MAKES A LITTLE PATH WITH BUTTONS...
THOSE BUTTONS MAY LOOK TINY, EVEN TO A LITTLE GIRL.
BUT NOT TO A FAIRY!
LOOK!
THESE WILL BE PERFECT FOR THE NEW WAGON I'VE BEEN WORKING ON!
TINKER BELL, I'M NOT CARRYING THIS HUMAN JUNK BACK TO CAMP!
!
BUT IT ISN'T JUST BUTTONS THAT TINK'S INTERESTED IN ANYMORE!

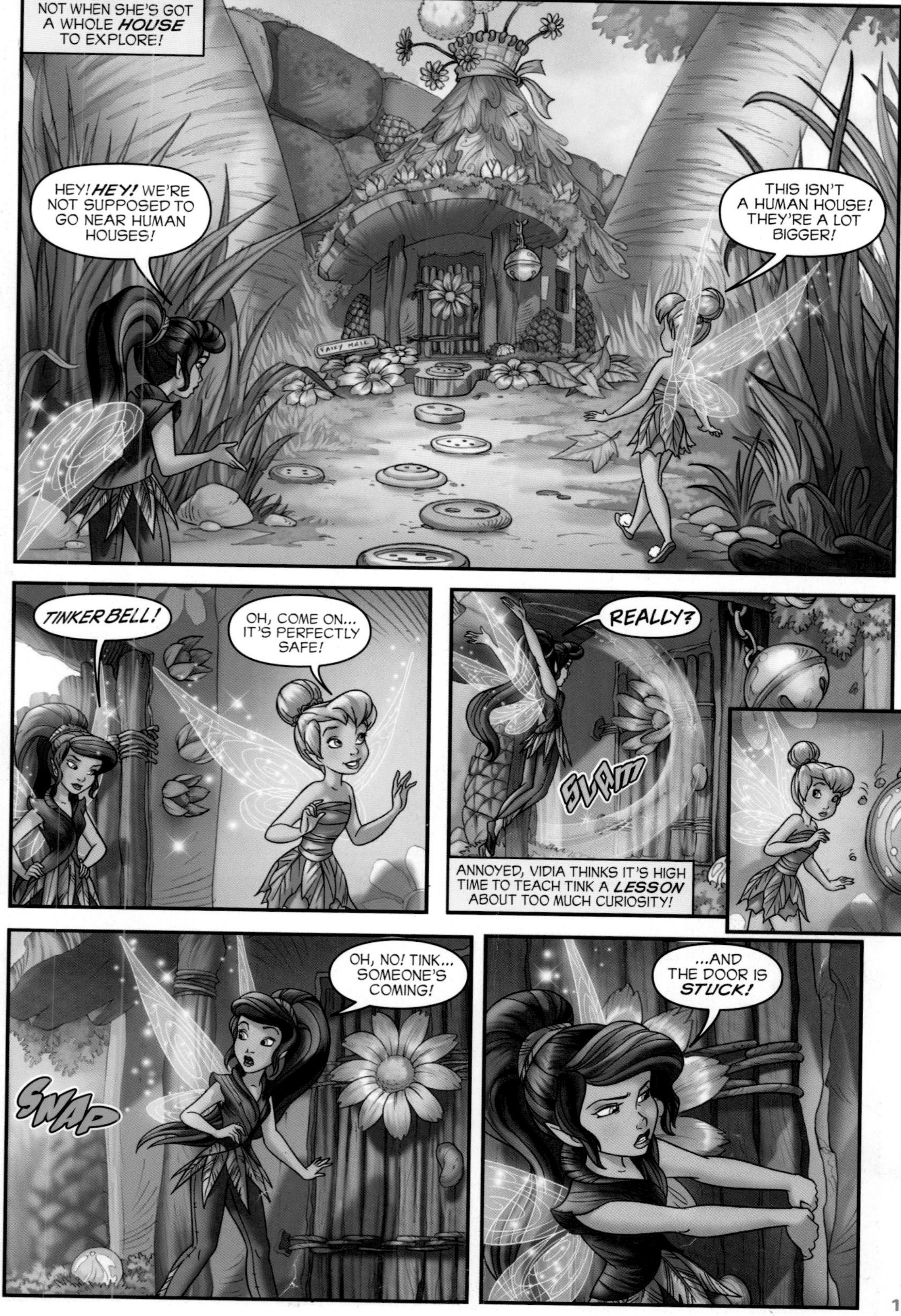
NOT WHEN SHE'S GOT A WHOLE HOUSE TO EXPLORE!
HEY! HEY! WE'RE NOT SUPPOSED TO GO NEAR HUMAN HOUSES!
THIS ISN'T A HUMAN HOUSE! THEY'RE A LOT BIGGER!
TINKER BELL!
OH, COME ON... IT'S PERFECTLY SAFE!
REALLY?
SLAM
ANNOYED, VIDIA THINKS IT'S HIGH TIME TO TEACH TINK A LESSON ABOUT TOO MUCH CURIOSITY!
OH, NO! TINK... SOMEONE'S COMING!
SNAP
...AND THE DOOR IS STUCK!

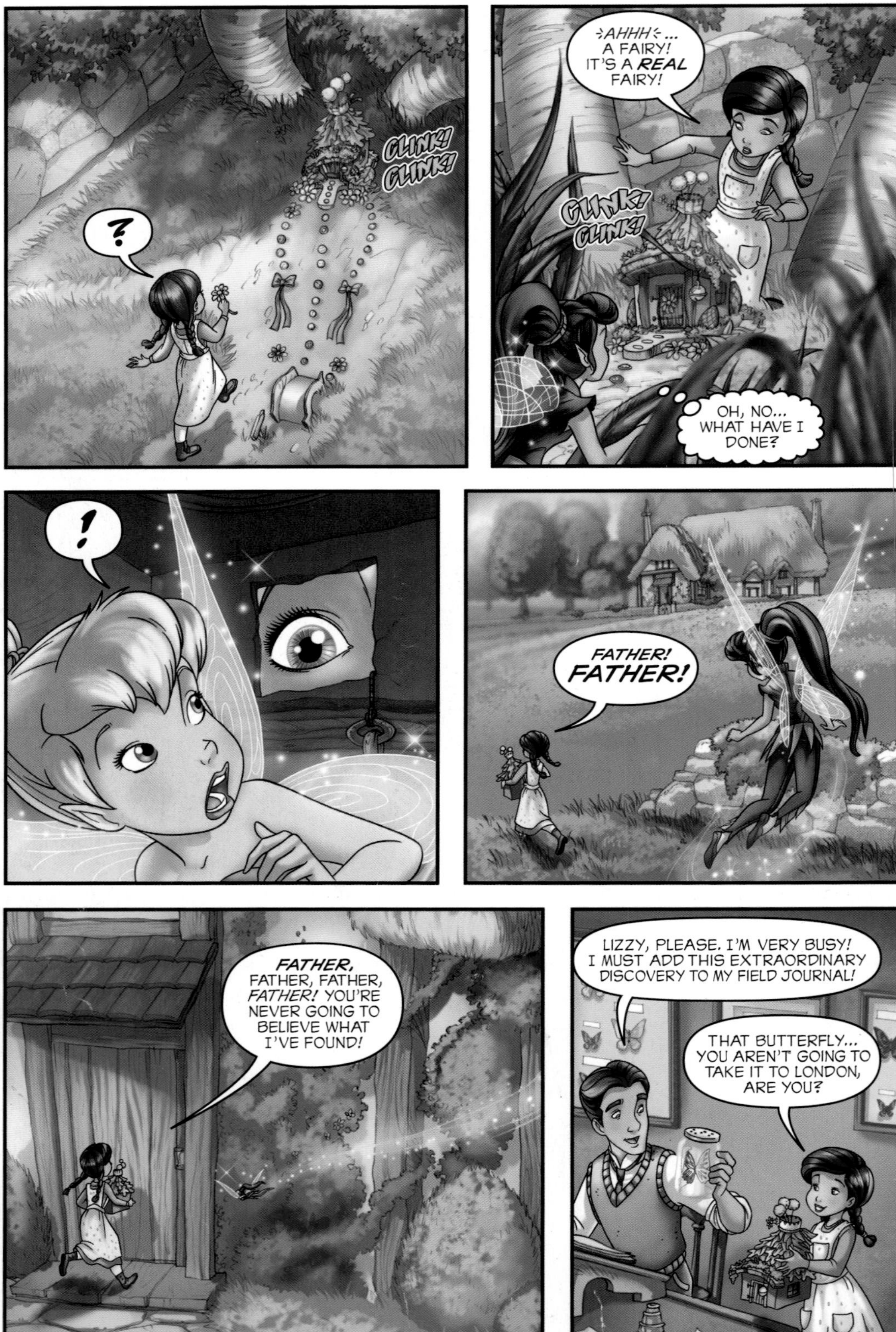
?
CLINK! CLINK!
AHHH... A FAIRY! IT'S A **REAL** FAIRY!
CLINK! CLINK!
OH, NO... WHAT HAVE I DONE?
!
FATHER! FATHER!
FATHER, FATHER, FATHER, *FATHER!* YOU'RE NEVER GOING TO BELIEVE WHAT I'VE FOUND!
LIZZY, PLEASE. I'M VERY BUSY! I MUST ADD THIS EXTRAORDINARY DISCOVERY TO MY FIELD JOURNAL!
THAT BUTTERFLY... YOU AREN'T GOING TO TAKE IT TO LONDON, ARE YOU?

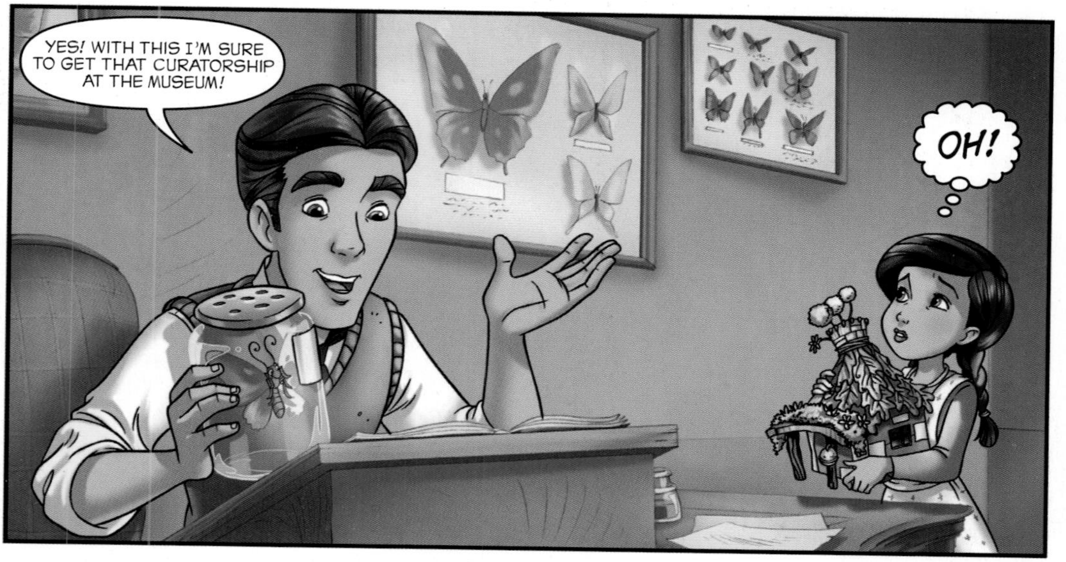
YES! WITH THIS I'M SURE TO GET THAT CURATORSHIP AT THE MUSEUM!
OH!

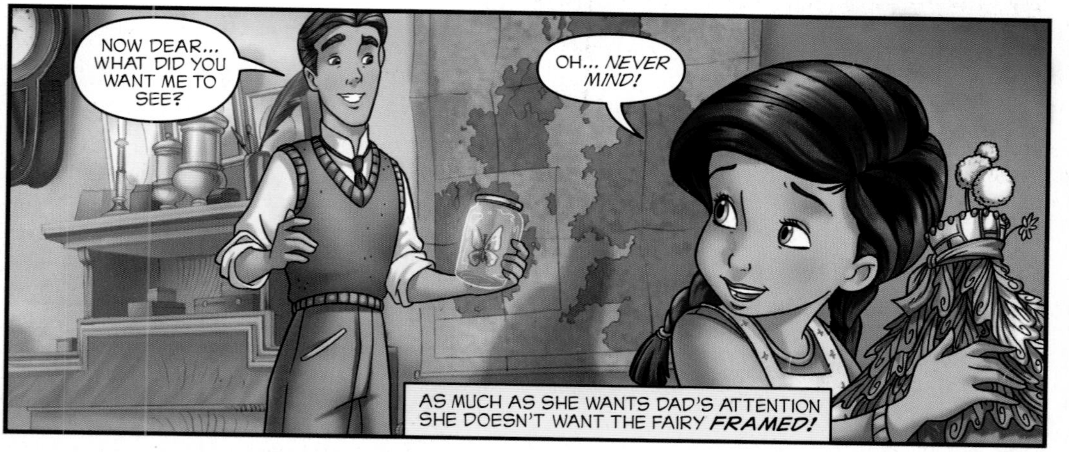
NOW DEAR... WHAT DID YOU WANT ME TO SEE?
OH... NEVER MIND!
AS MUCH AS SHE WANTS DAD'S ATTENTION SHE DOESN'T WANT THE FAIRY FRAMED!

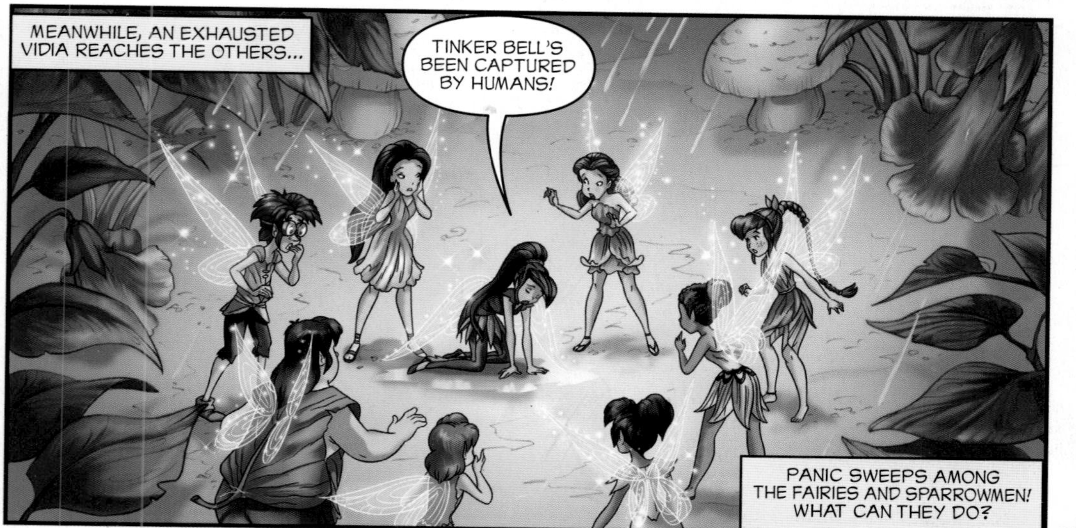
MEANWHILE, AN EXHAUSTED VIDIA REACHES THE OTHERS...
TINKER BELL'S BEEN CAPTURED BY HUMANS!
PANIC SWEEPS AMONG THE FAIRIES AND SPARROWMEN! WHAT CAN THEY DO?

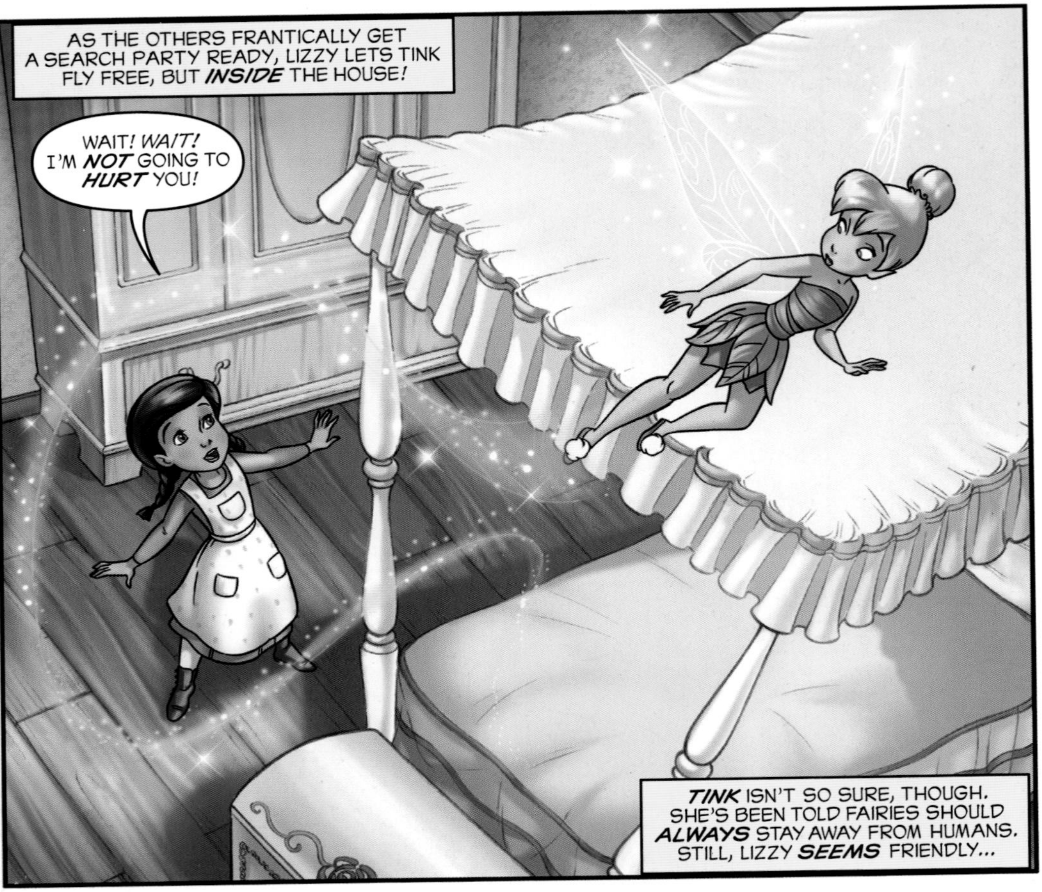
AS THE OTHERS FRANTICALLY GET A SEARCH PARTY READY, LIZZY LETS TINK FLY FREE, BUT INSIDE THE HOUSE!
WAIT! WAIT! I'M NOT GOING TO HURT YOU!
TINK ISN'T SO SURE, THOUGH. SHE'S BEEN TOLD FAIRIES SHOULD ALWAYS STAY AWAY FROM HUMANS. STILL, LIZZY SEEMS FRIENDLY...

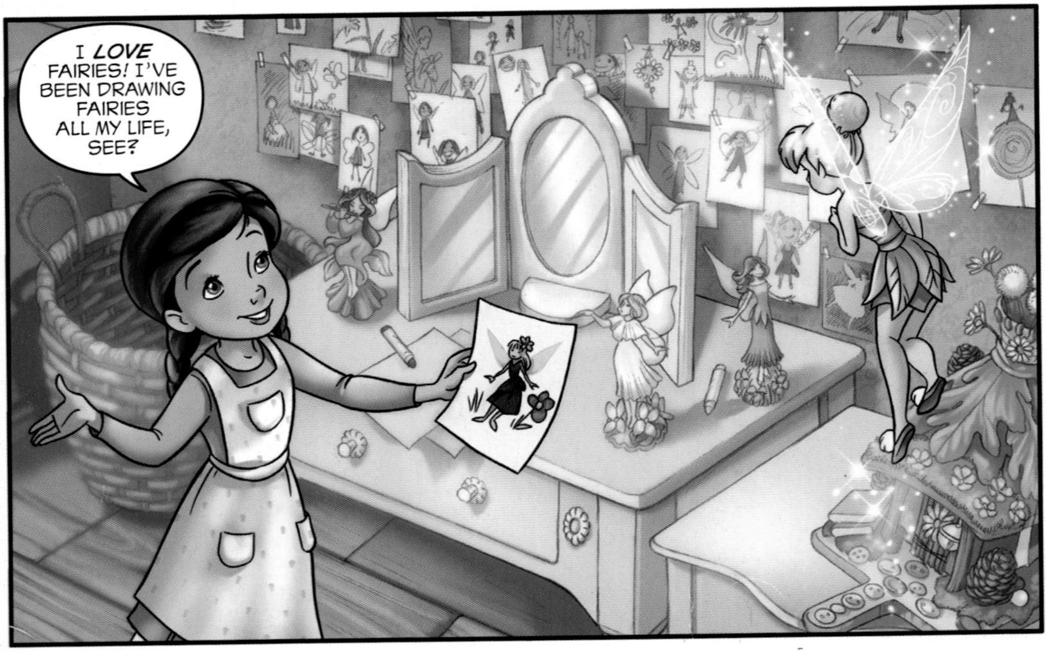
I LOVE FAIRIES! I'VE BEEN DRAWING FAIRIES ALL MY LIFE, SEE?

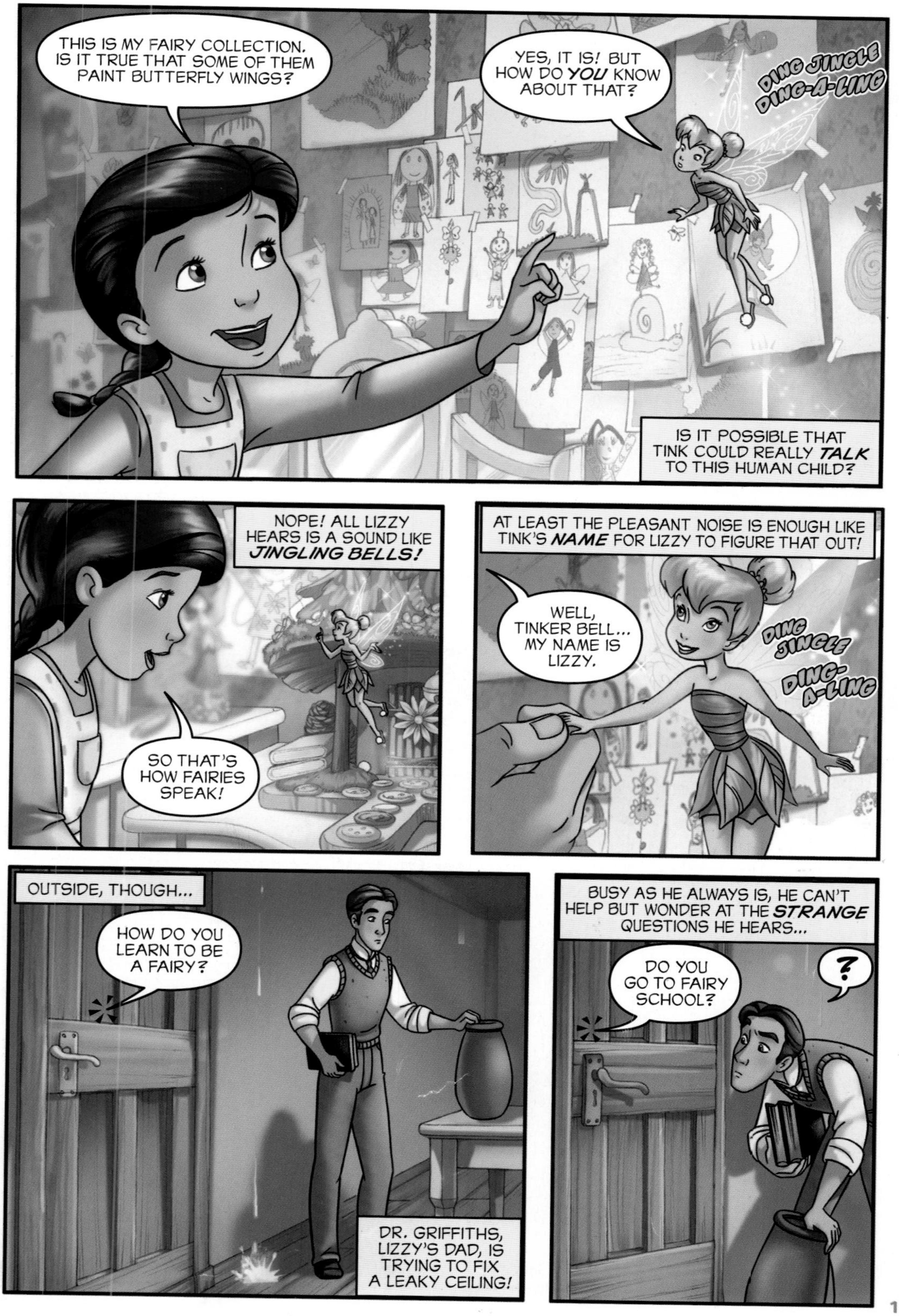

THIS IS MY FAIRY COLLECTION. IS IT TRUE THAT SOME OF THEM PAINT BUTTERFLY WINGS?
YES, IT IS! BUT HOW DO YOU KNOW ABOUT THAT?
DING JINGLE DING-A-LING
IS IT POSSIBLE THAT TINK COULD REALLY TALK TO THIS HUMAN CHILD?
NOPE! ALL LIZZY HEARS IS A SOUND LIKE JINGLING BELLS!
SO THAT'S HOW FAIRIES SPEAK!
AT LEAST THE PLEASANT NOISE IS ENOUGH LIKE TINK'S NAME FOR LIZZY TO FIGURE THAT OUT!
WELL, TINKER BELL... MY NAME IS LIZZY.
DING JINGLE
DING-A-LING
OUTSIDE, THOUGH...
HOW DO YOU LEARN TO BE A FAIRY?
DR. GRIFFITHS, LIZZY'S DAD, IS TRYING TO FIX A LEAKY CEILING!
BUSY AS HE ALWAYS IS, HE CAN'T HELP BUT WONDER AT THE STRANGE QUESTIONS HE HEARS...
DO YOU GO TO FAIRY SCHOOL?
?

SO OF COURSE HE *HAS* TO ASK...

LIZZY? WHO ARE YOU TALKING TO?

OH... *UM*...

MY DIARY!

OH, THAT'S NICE. LOOK, I BROUGHT YOU SOME OF *MY JOURNALS!*

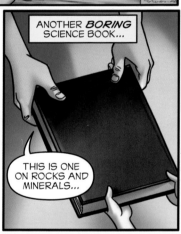

ANOTHER *BORING* SCIENCE BOOK...

THIS IS ONE ON ROCKS AND MINERALS...

SCIENCE IS GREAT AND ALL, BUT LIZZY HAS *OTHER* INTERESTS!

IS THERE ONE ABOUT *FAIRIES?*

OF COURSE NOT! THESE ARE BASED ON SCIENTIFIC FACTS!

AND, OF COURSE, SCIENTISTS DON'T BELIEVE IN FAIRIES!

ANYWAY, HERE'S A BLANK JOURNAL...FILL IT WITH YOUR OWN RESEARCH!

A *DRIPPING* SOUND TURNS DR. GRIFFITHS AWAY FROM HIS DAUGHTER.

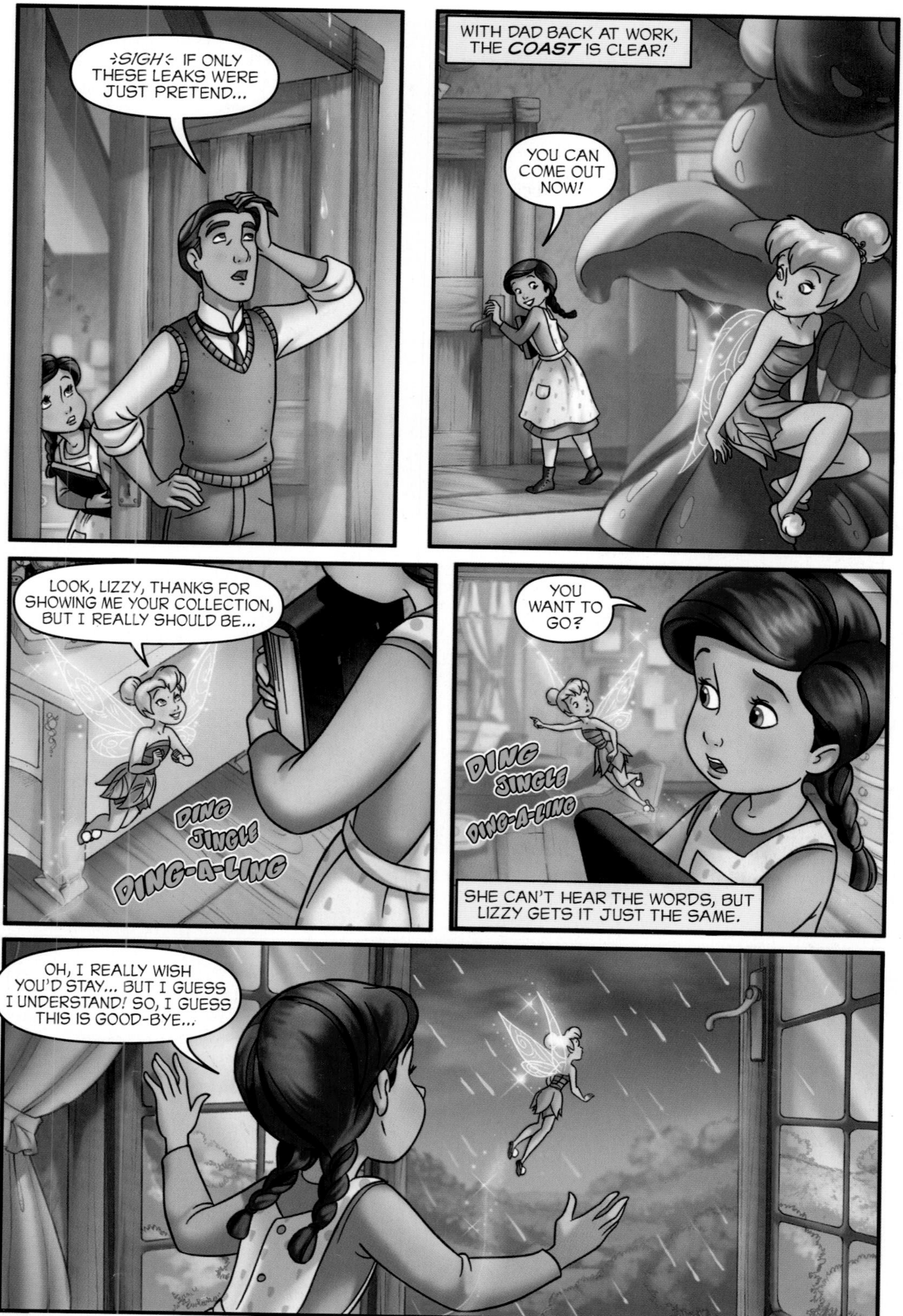

⊰SIGH⊱ IF ONLY THESE LEAKS WERE JUST PRETEND...
WITH DAD BACK AT WORK, THE COAST IS CLEAR!
YOU CAN COME OUT NOW!
LOOK, LIZZY, THANKS FOR SHOWING ME YOUR COLLECTION, BUT I REALLY SHOULD BE...
DING JINGLE DING-A-LING
YOU WANT TO GO?
DING JINGLE DING-A-LING
SHE CAN'T HEAR THE WORDS, BUT LIZZY GETS IT JUST THE SAME.
OH, I REALLY WISH YOU'D STAY... BUT I GUESS I UNDERSTAND! SO, I GUESS THIS IS GOOD-BYE...

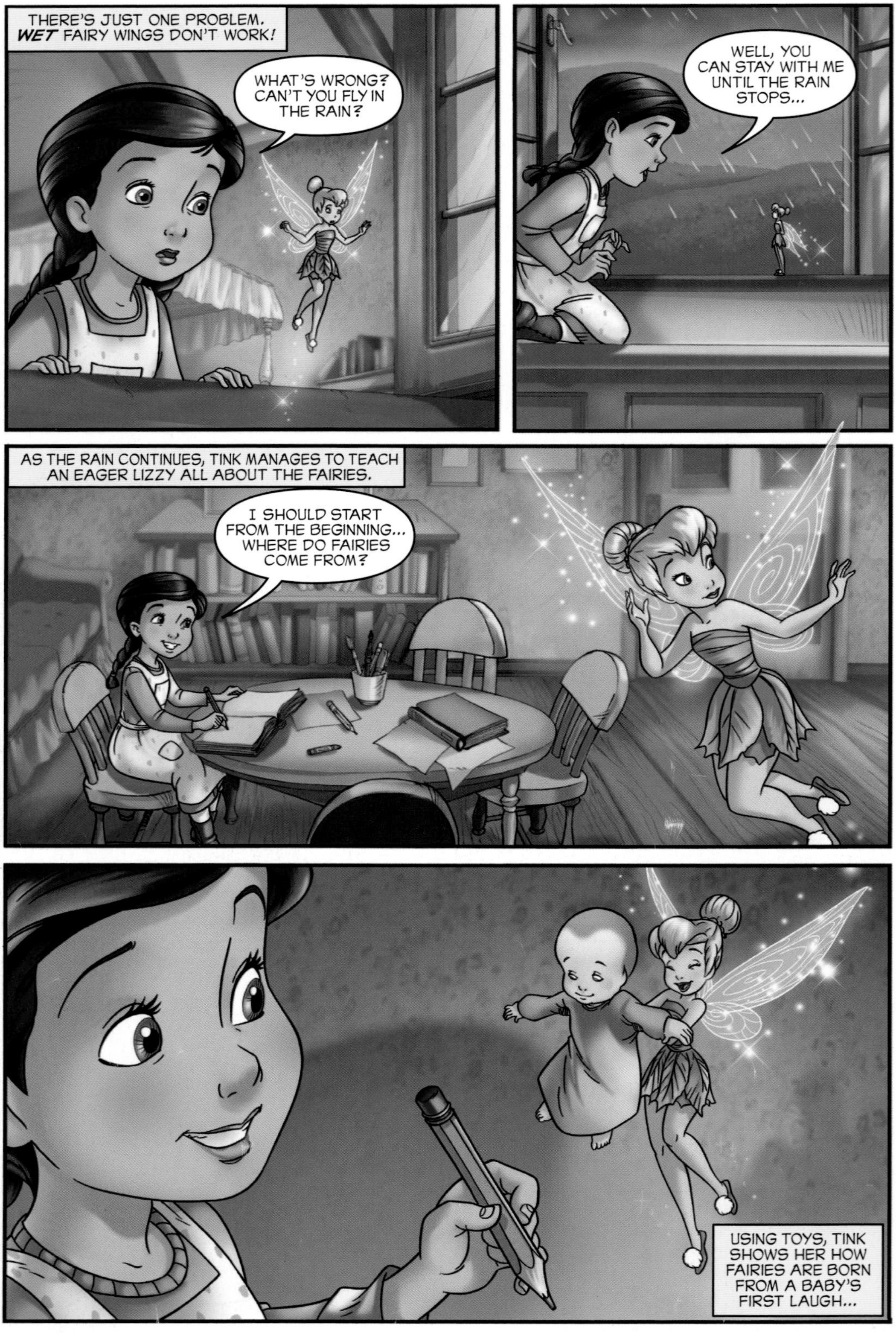
THERE'S JUST ONE PROBLEM. *WET* FAIRY WINGS DON'T WORK!
WHAT'S WRONG? CAN'T YOU FLY IN THE RAIN?
WELL, YOU CAN STAY WITH ME UNTIL THE RAIN STOPS...
AS THE RAIN CONTINUES, TINK MANAGES TO TEACH AN EAGER LIZZY ALL ABOUT THE FAIRIES.
I SHOULD START FROM THE BEGINNING... WHERE DO FAIRIES COME FROM?
USING TOYS, TINK SHOWS HER HOW FAIRIES ARE BORN FROM A BABY'S FIRST LAUGH...

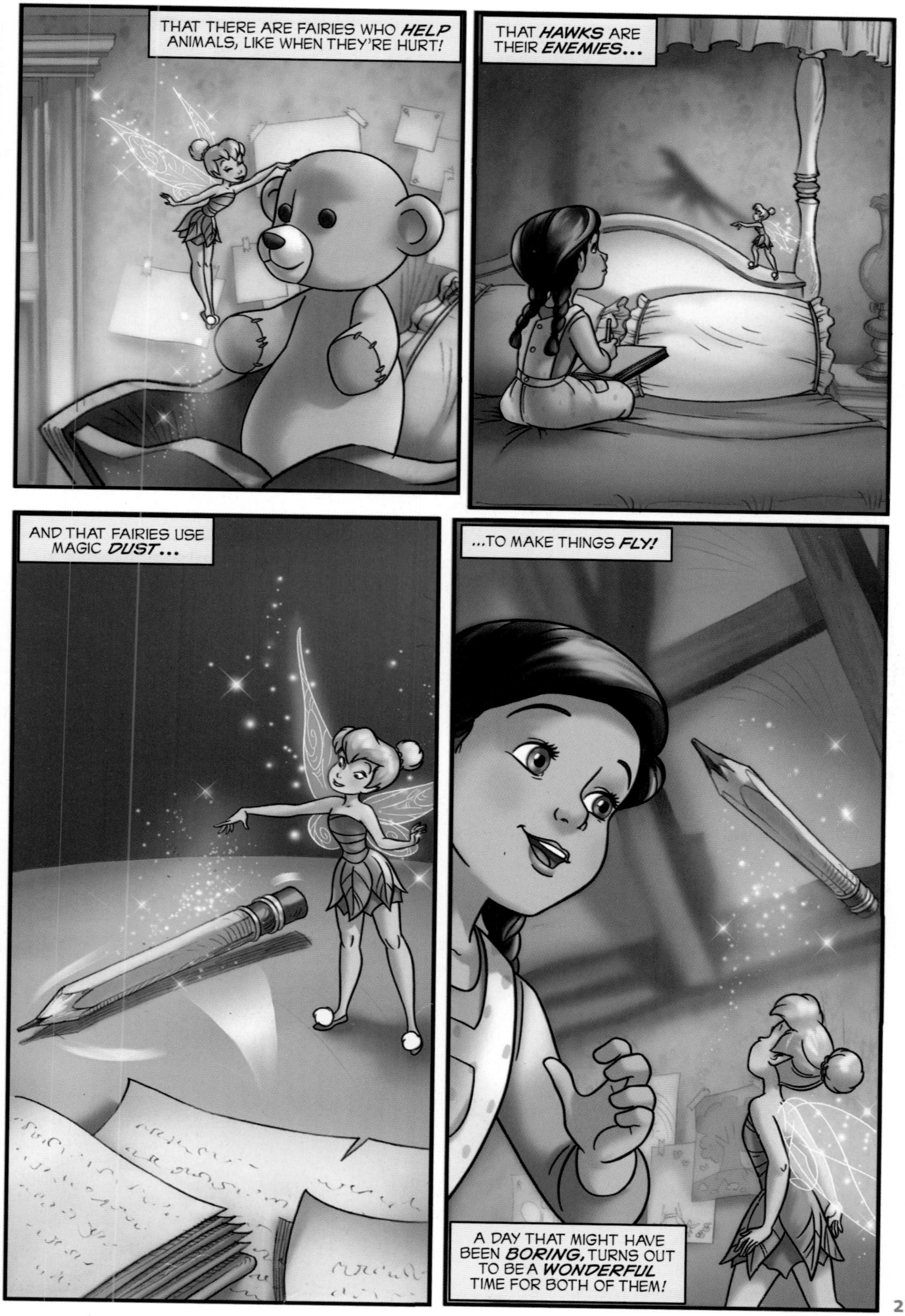
THAT THERE ARE FAIRIES WHO HELP ANIMALS, LIKE WHEN THEY'RE HURT!
THAT HAWKS ARE THEIR ENEMIES...
AND THAT FAIRIES USE MAGIC DUST...
...TO MAKE THINGS FLY!
A DAY THAT MIGHT HAVE BEEN BORING, TURNS OUT TO BE A WONDERFUL TIME FOR BOTH OF THEM!

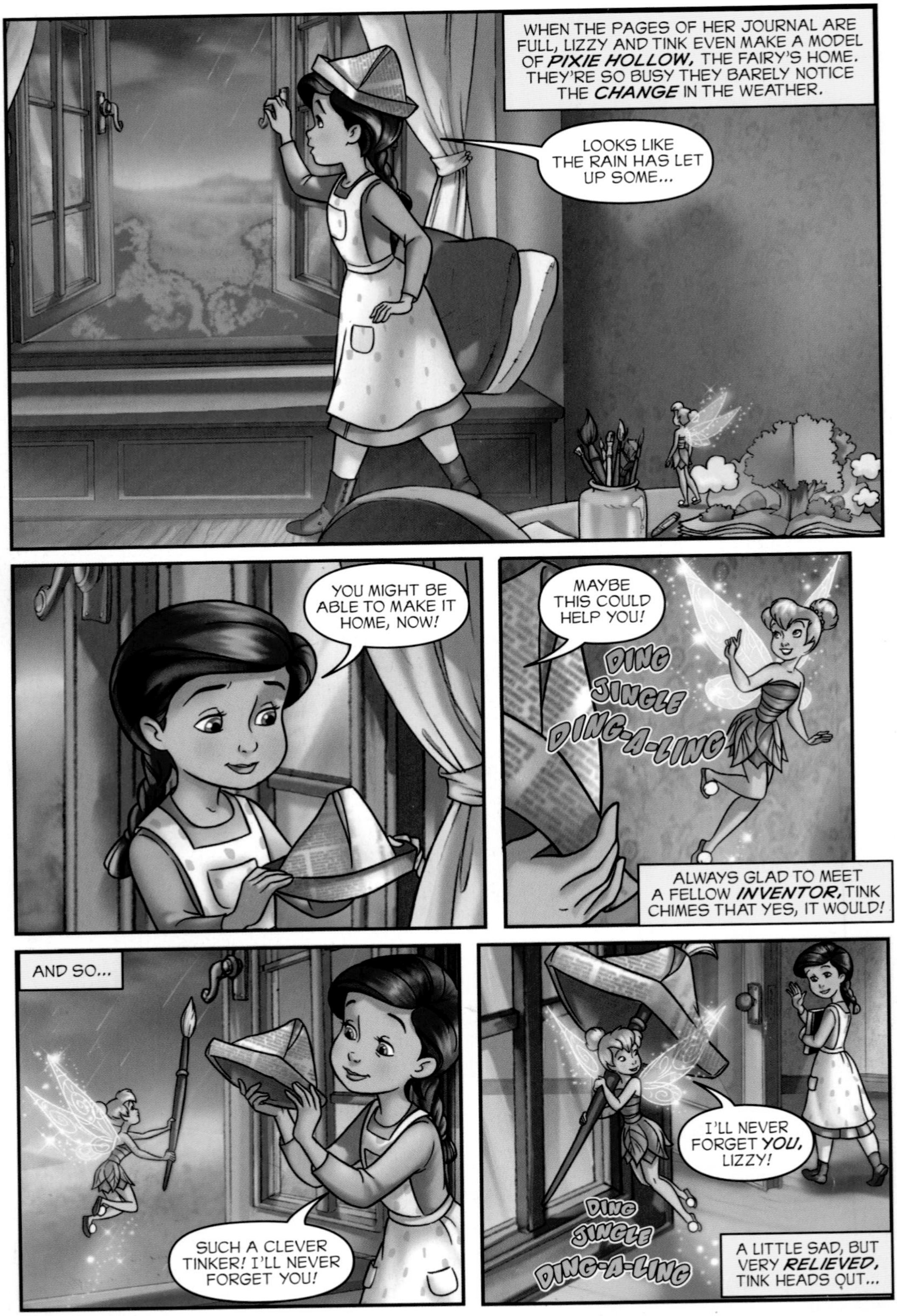
WHEN THE PAGES OF HER JOURNAL ARE FULL, LIZZY AND TINK EVEN MAKE A MODEL OF *PIXIE HOLLOW,* THE FAIRY'S HOME. THEY'RE SO BUSY THEY BARELY NOTICE THE *CHANGE* IN THE WEATHER.
LOOKS LIKE THE RAIN HAS LET UP SOME...
YOU MIGHT BE ABLE TO MAKE IT HOME, NOW!
MAYBE THIS COULD HELP YOU!
DING JINGLE DING-A-LING
ALWAYS GLAD TO MEET A FELLOW *INVENTOR,* TINK CHIMES THAT YES, IT WOULD!
AND SO...
SUCH A CLEVER TINKER! I'LL NEVER FORGET YOU!
I'LL NEVER FORGET *YOU,* LIZZY!
DING JINGLE DING-A-LING
A LITTLE SAD, BUT VERY *RELIEVED,* TINK HEADS OUT...

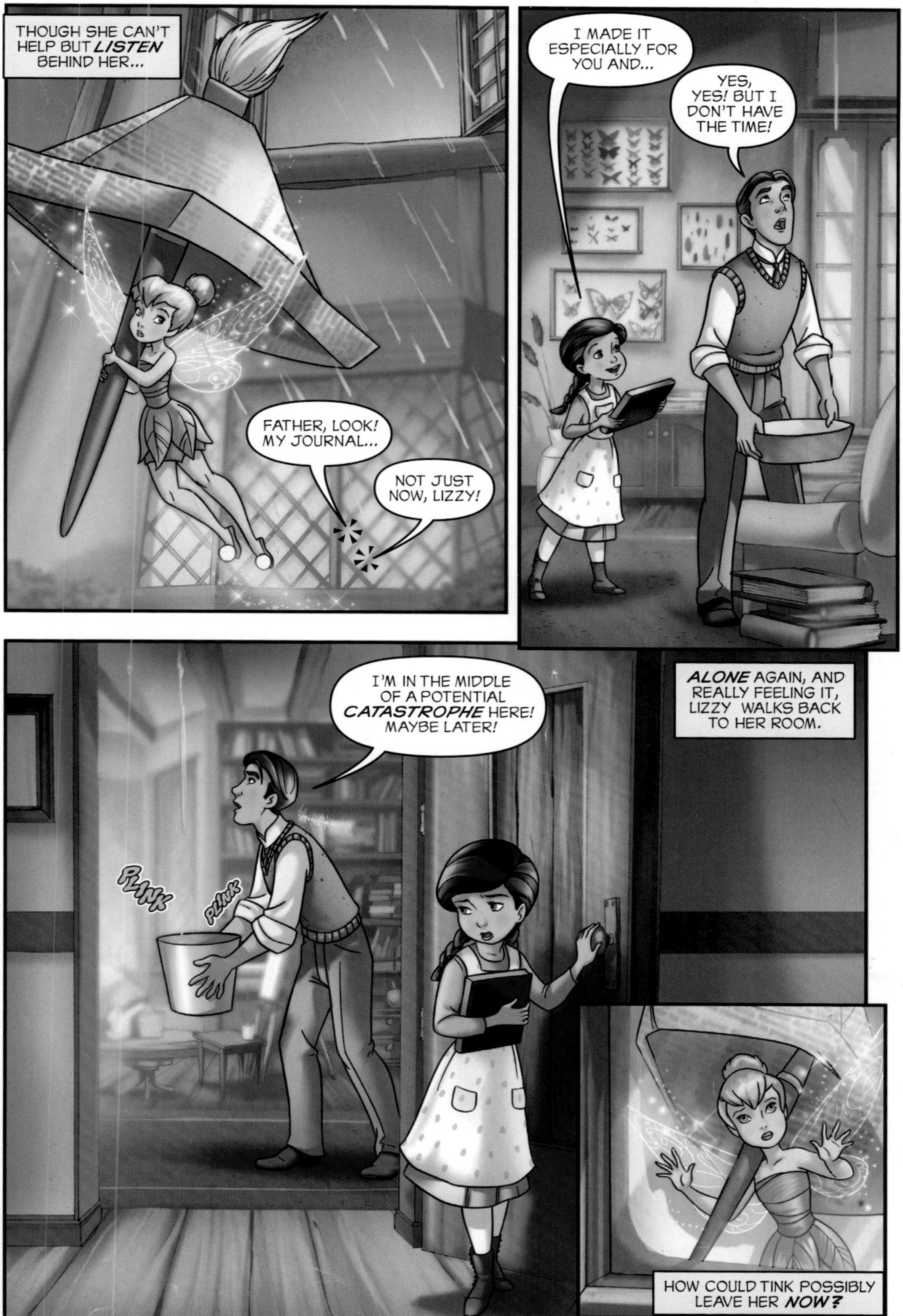
THOUGH SHE CAN'T HELP BUT LISTEN BEHIND HER...
FATHER, LOOK! MY JOURNAL...
NOT JUST NOW, LIZZY!
I MADE IT ESPECIALLY FOR YOU AND...
YES, YES! BUT I DON'T HAVE THE TIME!
I'M IN THE MIDDLE OF A POTENTIAL CATASTROPHE HERE! MAYBE LATER!
ALONE AGAIN, AND REALLY FEELING IT, LIZZY WALKS BACK TO HER ROOM.
PLINK
PLINK
HOW COULD TINK POSSIBLY LEAVE HER NOW?

HER FATHER'S *OFTEN* BUSY, BUT IT NEVER GETS EASIER FOR LIZZY. IT'S ESPECIALLY HARD TO BE ALONE WHEN YOU HAVE SO *MUCH* TO SHARE!

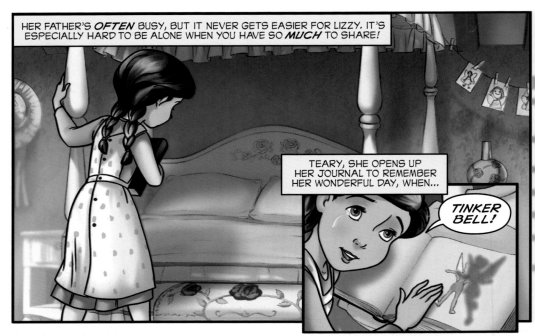

TEARY, SHE OPENS UP HER JOURNAL TO REMEMBER HER WONDERFUL DAY, WHEN...

TINKER BELL!

YOU CAME BACK!

I'M SO GLAD TO SEE YOU!

BUT... OH, TINK! FATHER HAS NO TIME FOR THE JOURNAL...

I THINK I CAN *FIX* THAT!

DING JINGLE DING-A-LING

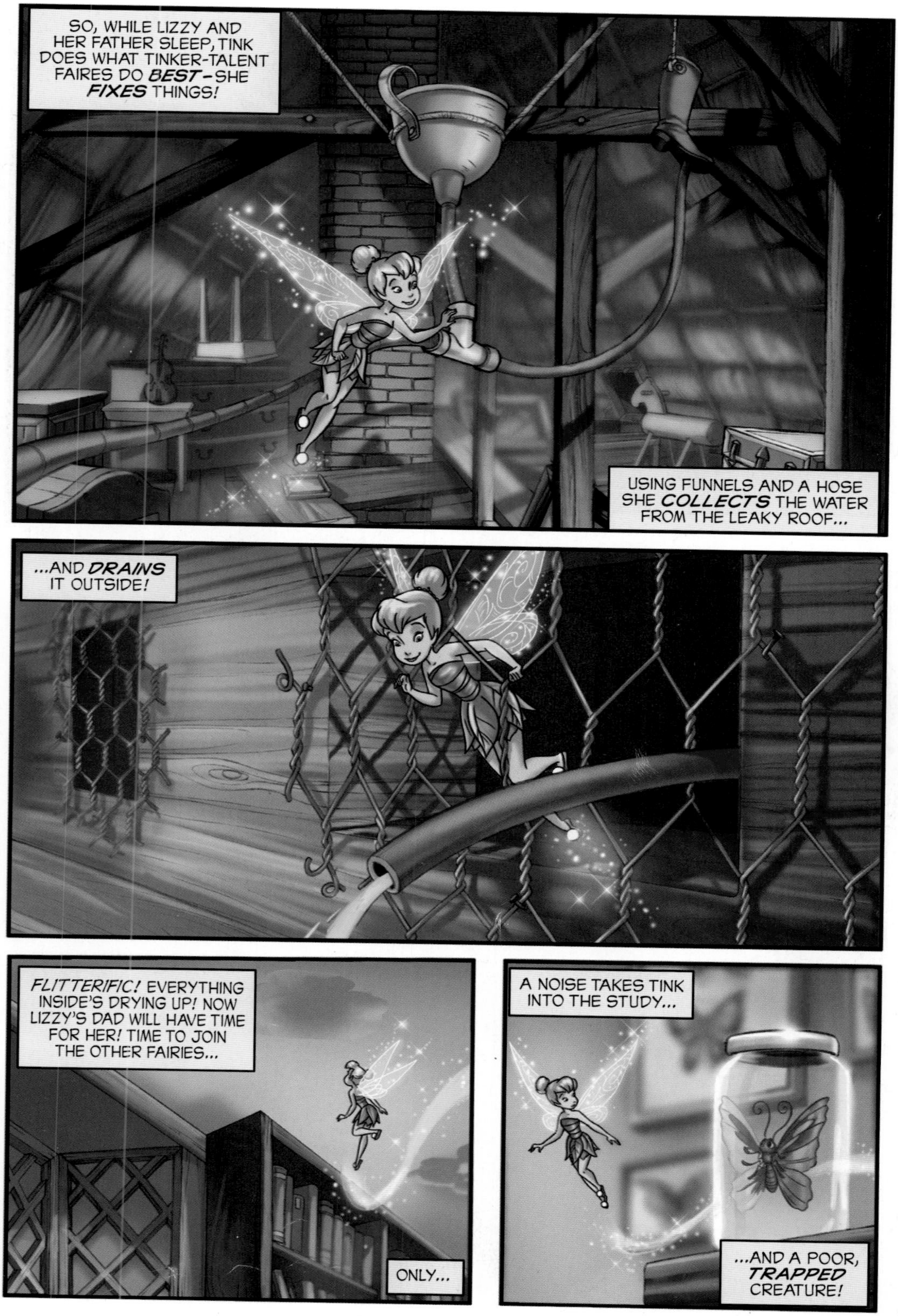
SO, WHILE LIZZY AND HER FATHER SLEEP, TINK DOES WHAT TINKER-TALENT FAIRES DO **BEST** – SHE **FIXES** THINGS!
USING FUNNELS AND A HOSE SHE **COLLECTS** THE WATER FROM THE LEAKY ROOF...
...AND **DRAINS** IT OUTSIDE!
FLITTERIFIC! EVERYTHING INSIDE'S DRYING UP! NOW LIZZY'S DAD WILL HAVE TIME FOR HER! TIME TO JOIN THE OTHER FAIRIES...
ONLY...
A NOISE TAKES TINK INTO THE STUDY...
...AND A POOR, **TRAPPED** CREATURE!

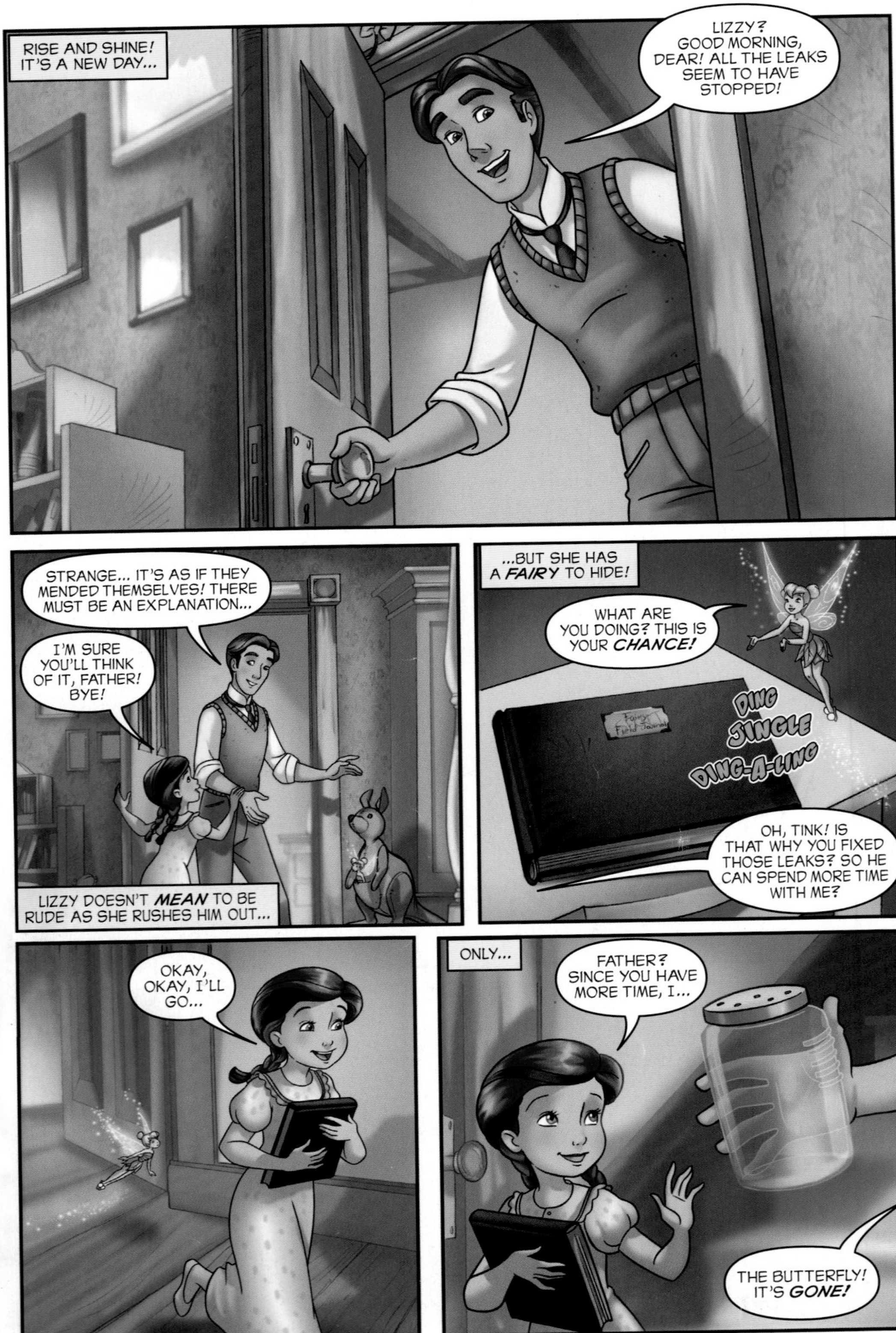

RISE AND SHINE! IT'S A NEW DAY...
LIZZY? GOOD MORNING, DEAR! ALL THE LEAKS SEEM TO HAVE STOPPED!
STRANGE... IT'S AS IF THEY MENDED THEMSELVES! THERE MUST BE AN EXPLANATION...
I'M SURE YOU'LL THINK OF IT, FATHER! BYE!
LIZZY DOESN'T MEAN TO BE RUDE AS SHE RUSHES HIM OUT...
...BUT SHE HAS A FAIRY TO HIDE!
WHAT ARE YOU DOING? THIS IS YOUR CHANCE!
DING
JINGLE
DING-A-LING
OH, TINK! IS THAT WHY YOU FIXED THOSE LEAKS? SO HE CAN SPEND MORE TIME WITH ME?
OKAY, OKAY, I'LL GO...
ONLY...
FATHER? SINCE YOU HAVE MORE TIME, I...
THE BUTTERFLY! IT'S GONE!

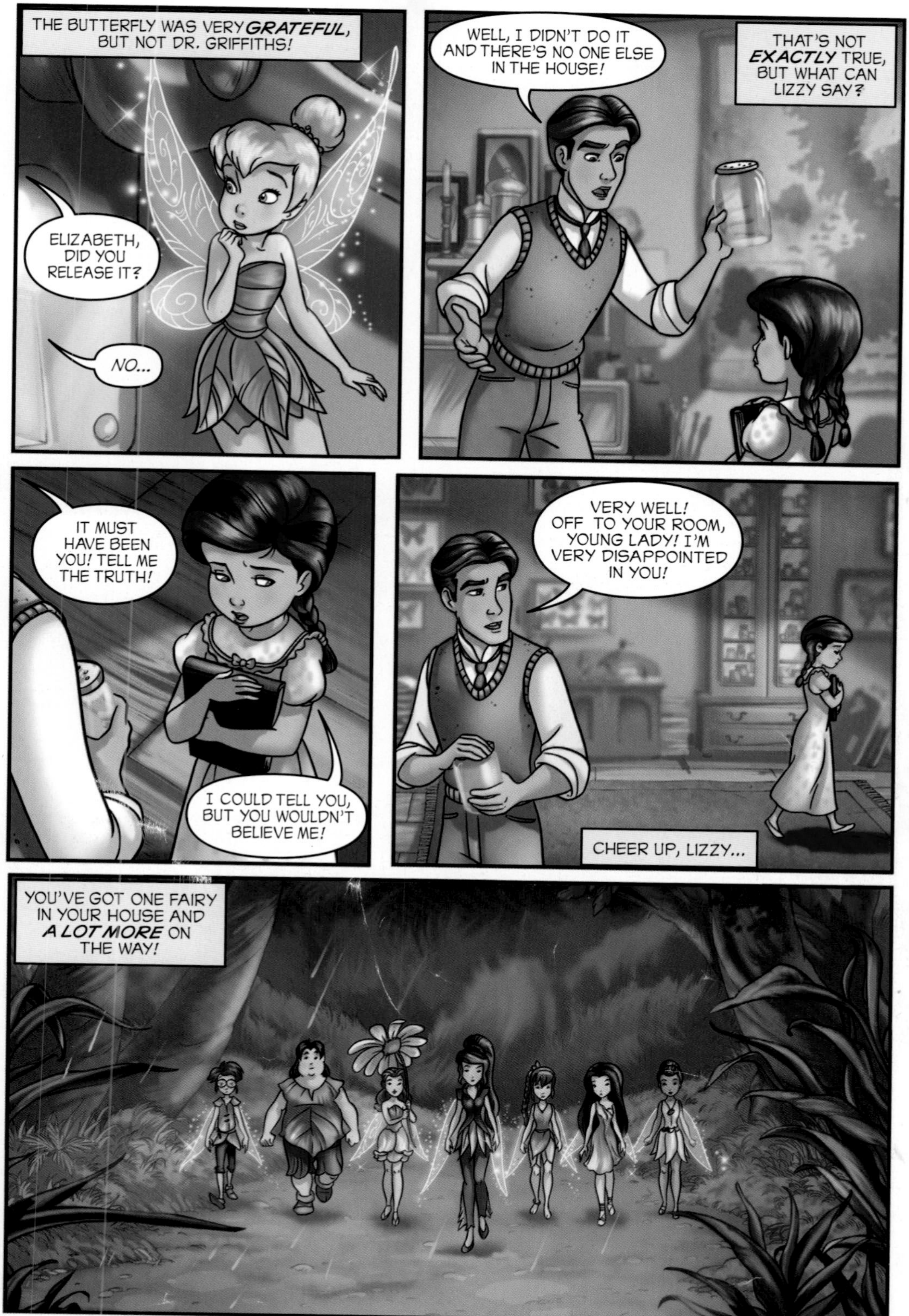
THE BUTTERFLY WAS VERY GRATEFUL, BUT NOT DR. GRIFFITHS!
ELIZABETH, DID YOU RELEASE IT?
NO...
WELL, I DIDN'T DO IT AND THERE'S NO ONE ELSE IN THE HOUSE!
THAT'S NOT EXACTLY TRUE, BUT WHAT CAN LIZZY SAY?
IT MUST HAVE BEEN YOU! TELL ME THE TRUTH!
I COULD TELL YOU, BUT YOU WOULDN'T BELIEVE ME!
VERY WELL! OFF TO YOUR ROOM, YOUNG LADY! I'M VERY DISAPPOINTED IN YOU!
CHEER UP, LIZZY...
YOU'VE GOT ONE FAIRY IN YOUR HOUSE AND A LOT MORE ON THE WAY!

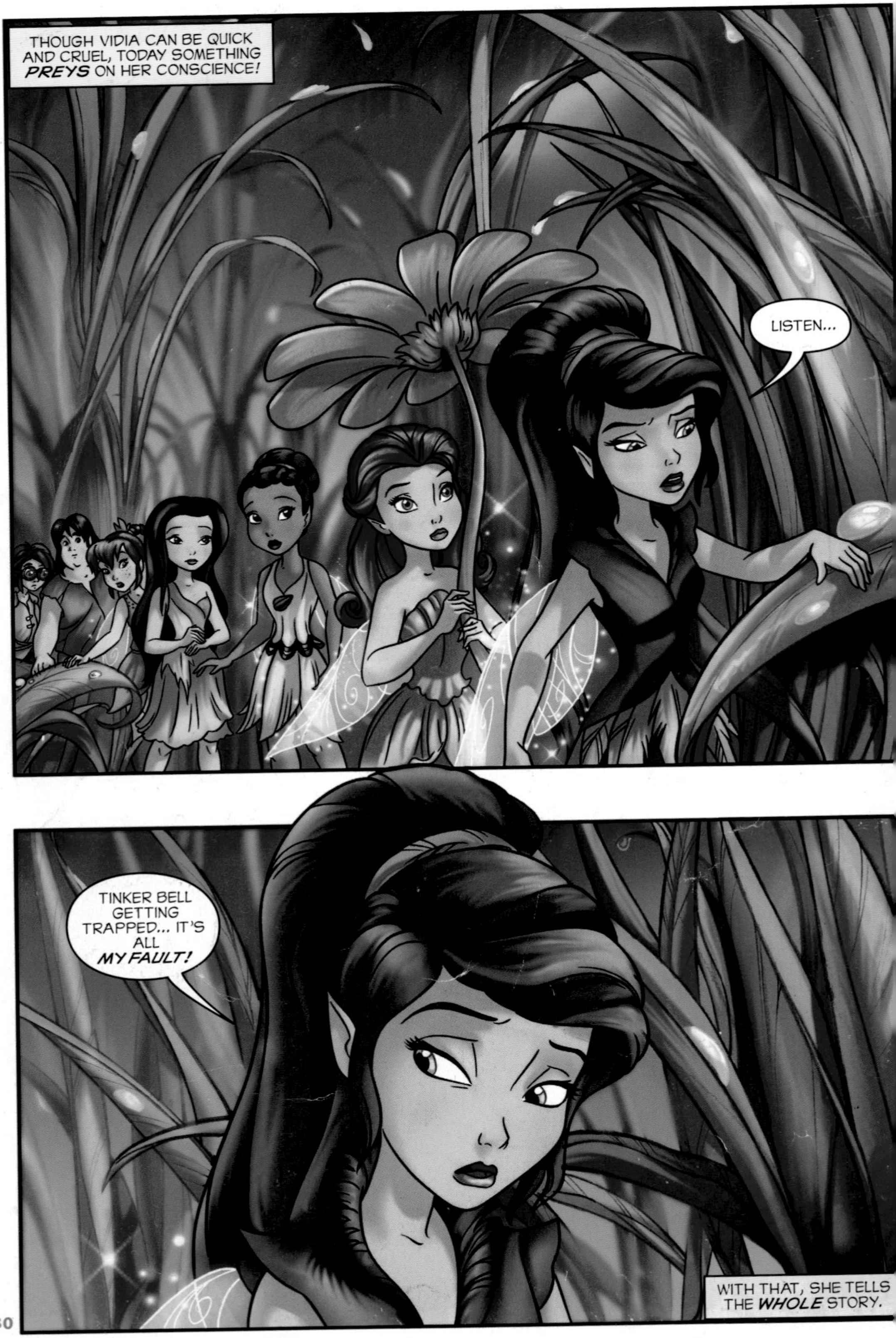
THOUGH VIDIA CAN BE QUICK AND CRUEL, TODAY SOMETHING PREYS ON HER CONSCIENCE!
LISTEN...
TINKER BELL GETTING TRAPPED... IT'S ALL MY FAULT!
WITH THAT, SHE TELLS THE WHOLE STORY.

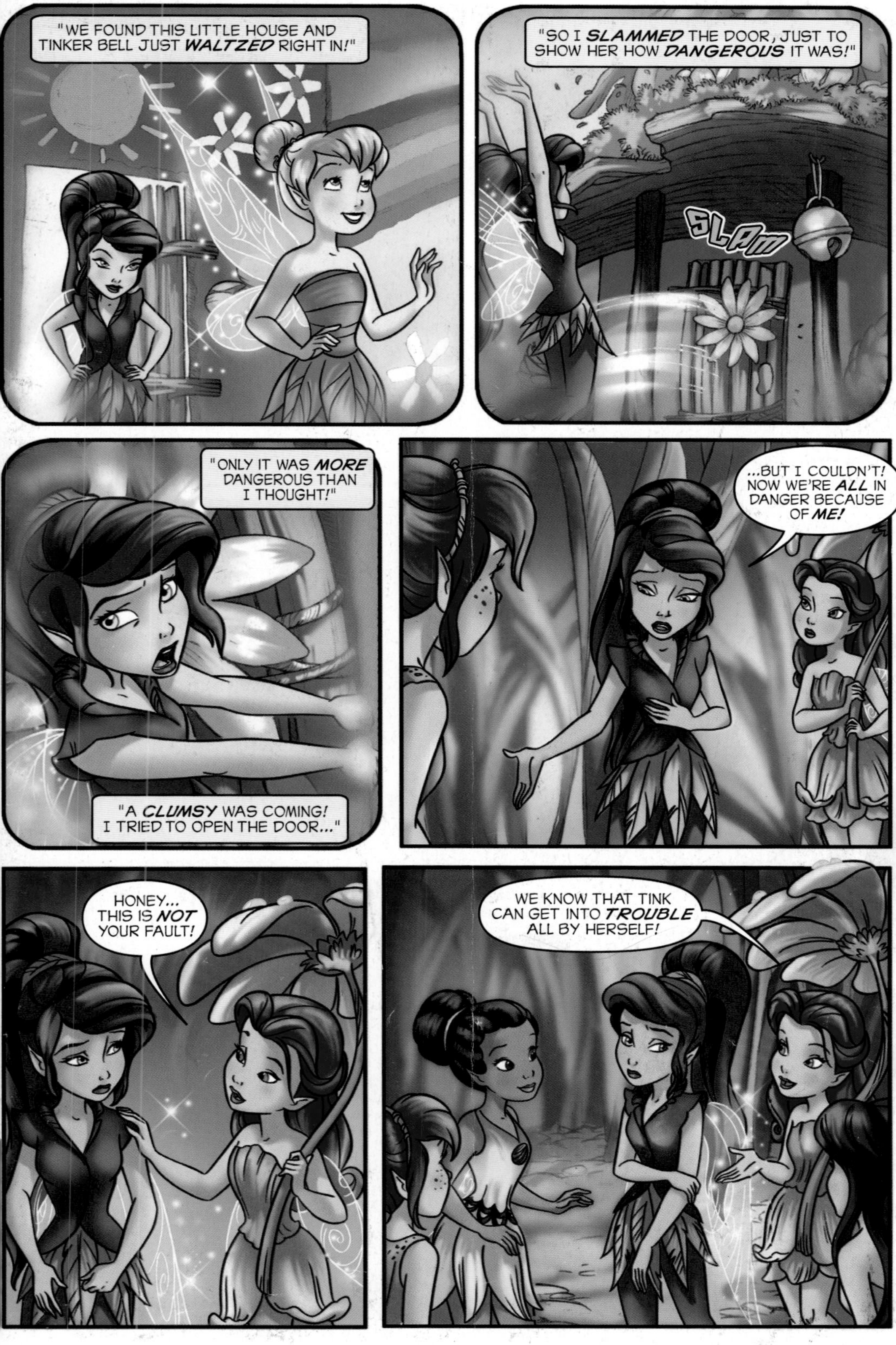

"WE FOUND THIS LITTLE HOUSE AND TINKER BELL JUST WALTZED RIGHT IN!"
"SO I SLAMMED THE DOOR, JUST TO SHOW HER HOW DANGEROUS IT WAS!"
SLAM
"ONLY IT WAS MORE DANGEROUS THAN I THOUGHT!"
"A CLUMSY WAS COMING! I TRIED TO OPEN THE DOOR..."
...BUT I COULDN'T! NOW WE'RE ALL IN DANGER BECAUSE OF ME!
HONEY... THIS IS NOT YOUR FAULT!
WE KNOW THAT TINK CAN GET INTO TROUBLE ALL BY HERSELF!

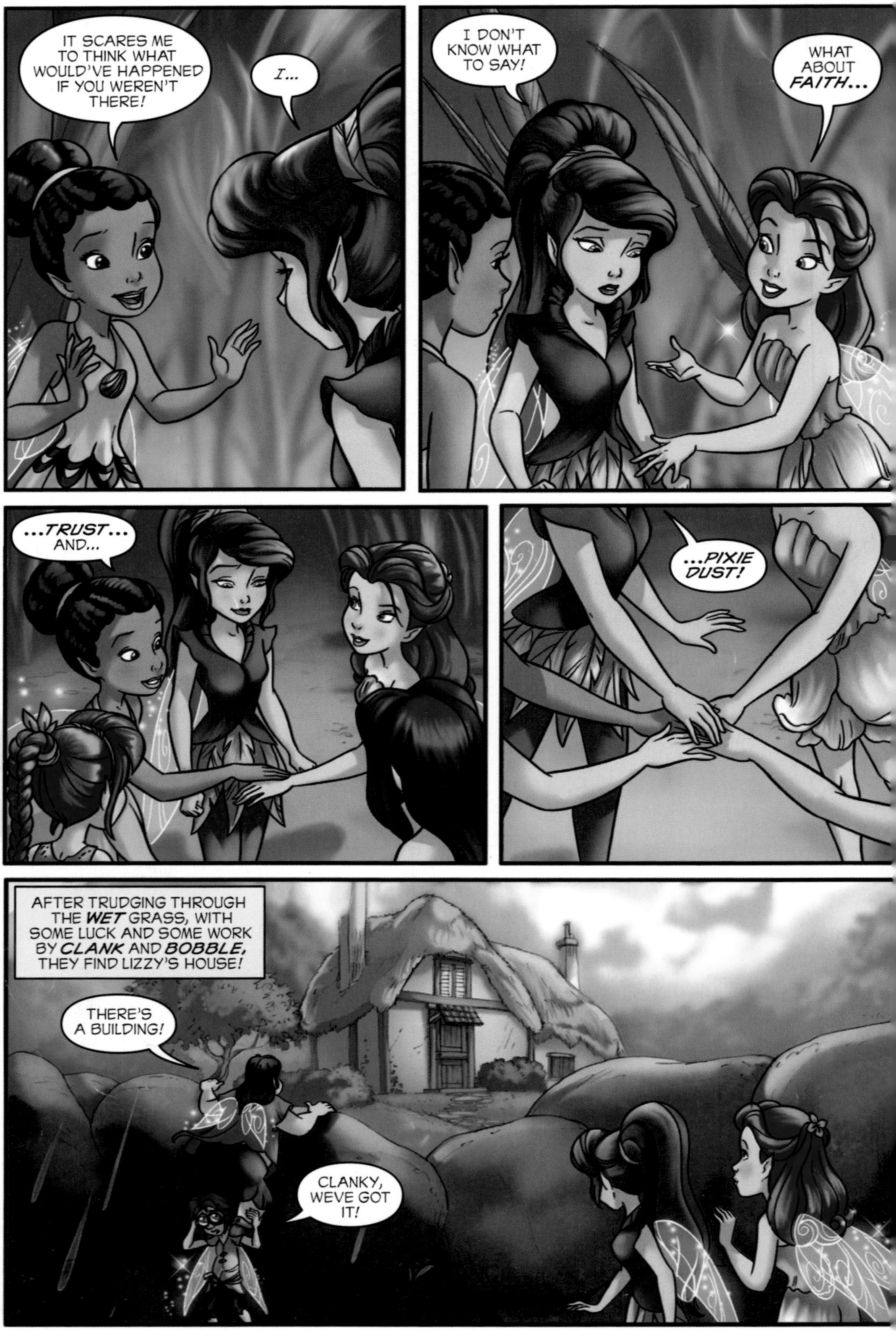
IT SCARES ME TO THINK WHAT WOULD'VE HAPPENED IF YOU WEREN'T THERE!
I...
I DON'T KNOW WHAT TO SAY!
WHAT ABOUT FAITH...
...TRUST... AND...
...PIXIE DUST!
AFTER TRUDGING THROUGH THE WET GRASS, WITH SOME LUCK AND SOME WORK BY CLANK AND BOBBLE, THEY FIND LIZZY'S HOUSE!
THERE'S A BUILDING!
CLANKY, WEVE GOT IT!

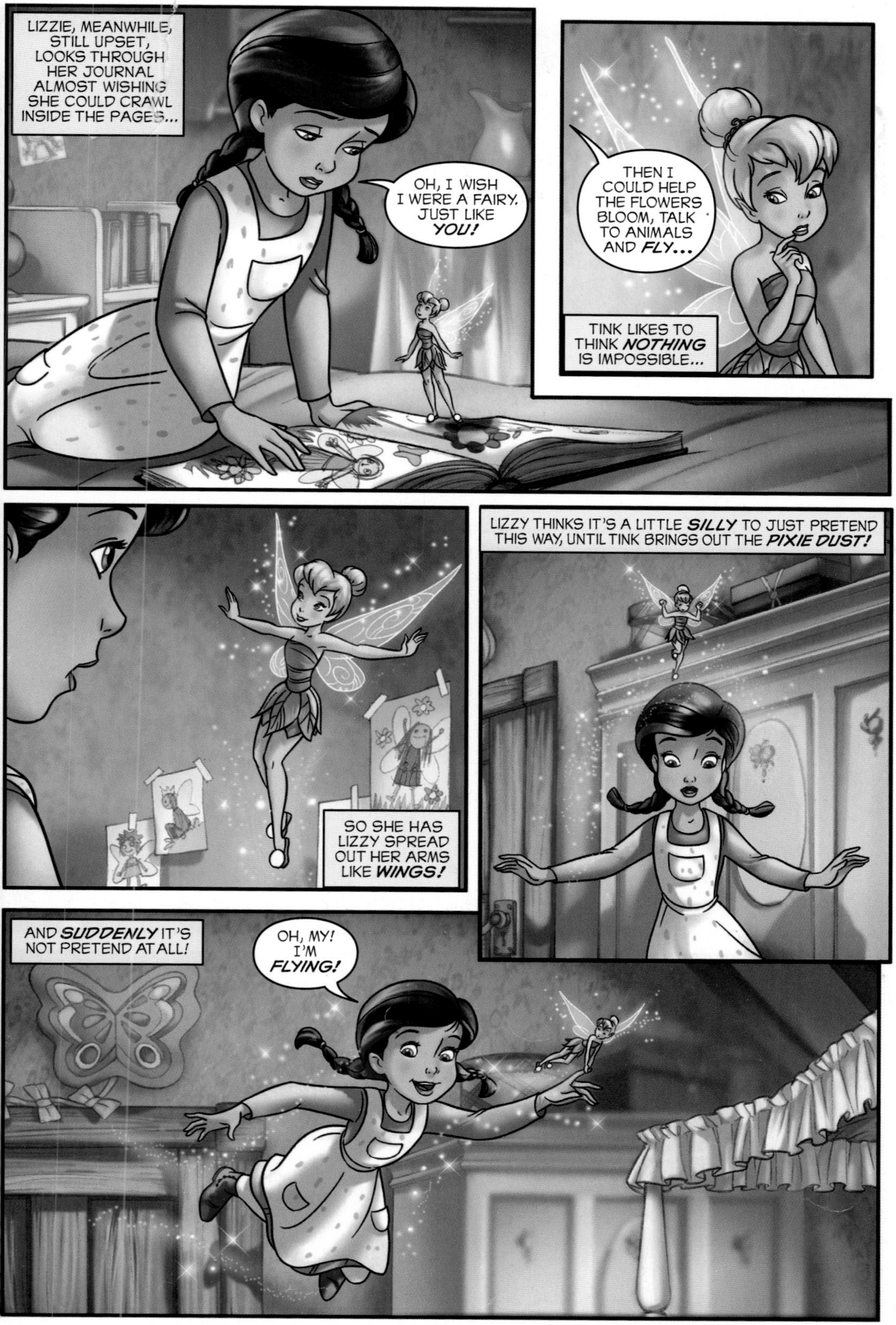

LIZZIE, MEANWHILE, STILL UPSET, LOOKS THROUGH HER JOURNAL ALMOST WISHING SHE COULD CRAWL INSIDE THE PAGES...
OH, I WISH I WERE A FAIRY. JUST LIKE YOU!
THEN I COULD HELP THE FLOWERS BLOOM, TALK TO ANIMALS AND FLY...
TINK LIKES TO THINK NOTHING IS IMPOSSIBLE...
SO SHE HAS LIZZY SPREAD OUT HER ARMS LIKE WINGS!
LIZZY THINKS IT'S A LITTLE SILLY TO JUST PRETEND THIS WAY, UNTIL TINK BRINGS OUT THE PIXIE DUST!
AND SUDDENLY IT'S NOT PRETEND AT ALL!
OH, MY! I'M FLYING!

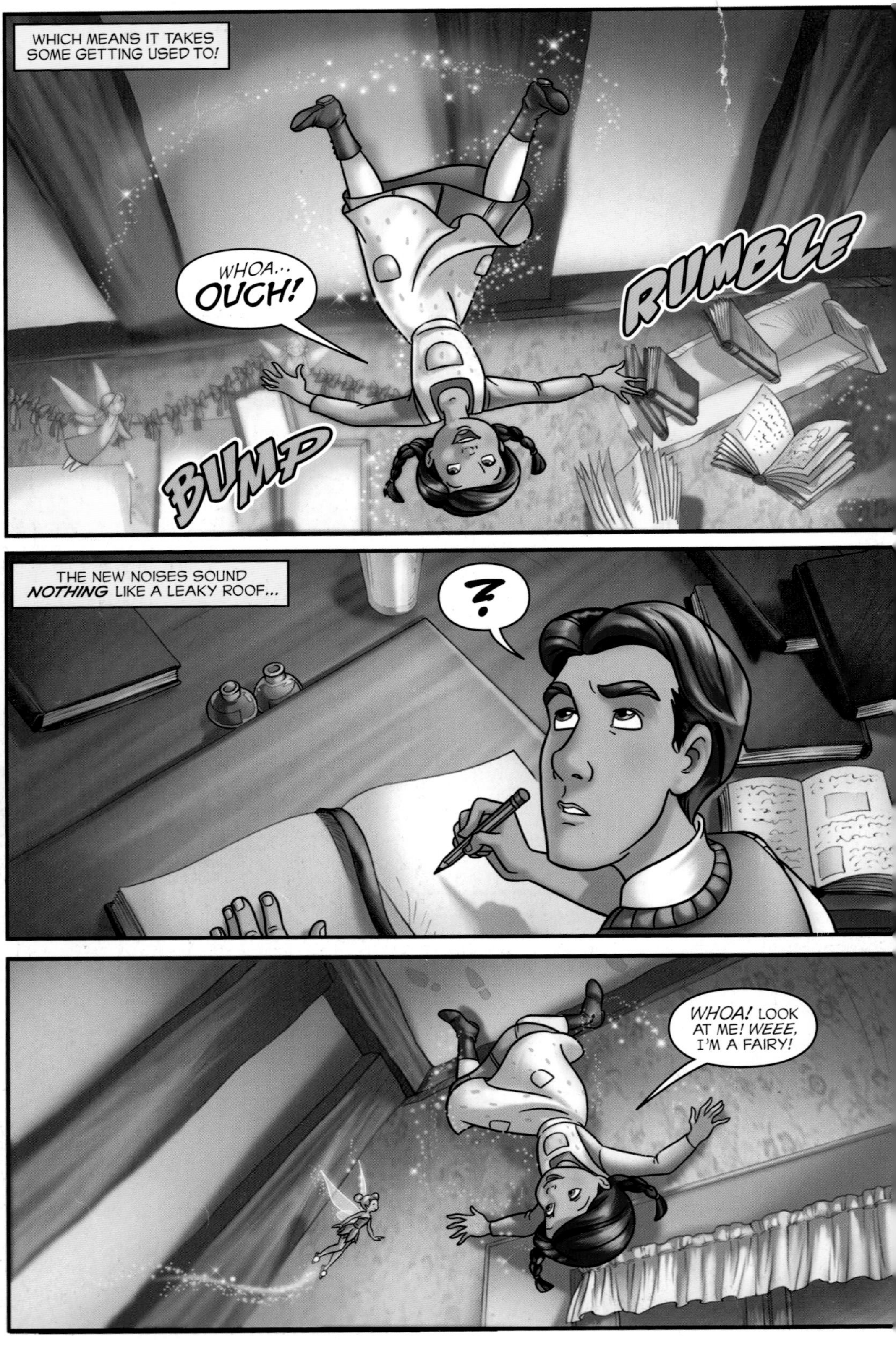
WHICH MEANS IT TAKES SOME GETTING USED TO!
WHOA... OUCH!
RUMBLE
BUMP
THE NEW NOISES SOUND NOTHING LIKE A LEAKY ROOF...
?
WHOA! LOOK AT ME! WEEE, I'M A FAIRY!

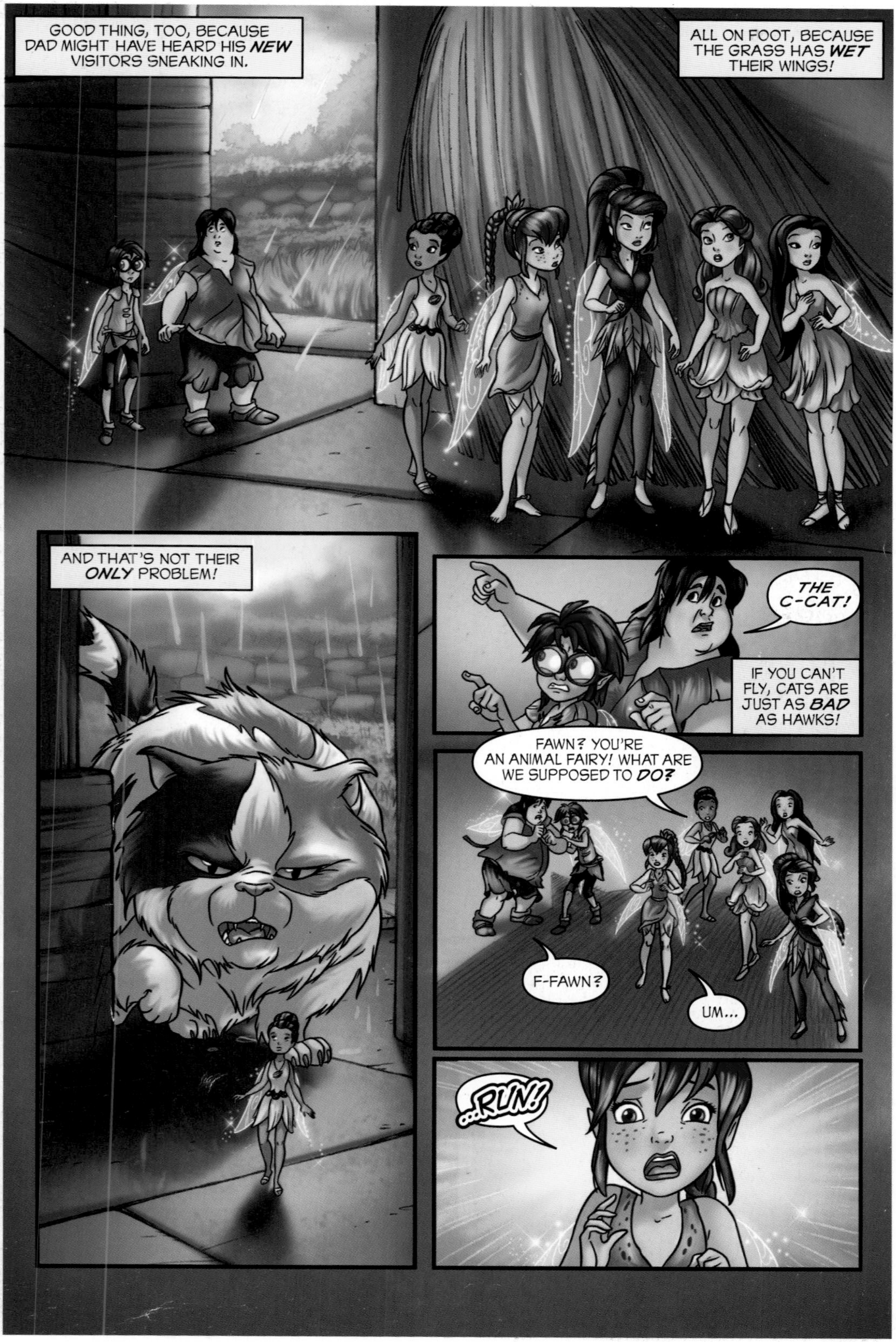
GOOD THING, TOO, BECAUSE DAD MIGHT HAVE HEARD HIS NEW VISITORS SNEAKING IN.
ALL ON FOOT, BECAUSE THE GRASS HAS WET THEIR WINGS!
AND THAT'S NOT THEIR ONLY PROBLEM!
THE C-CAT!
IF YOU CAN'T FLY, CATS ARE JUST AS BAD AS HAWKS!
FAWN? YOU'RE AN ANIMAL FAIRY! WHAT ARE WE SUPPOSED TO DO?
F-FAWN?
UM...
...RUN!

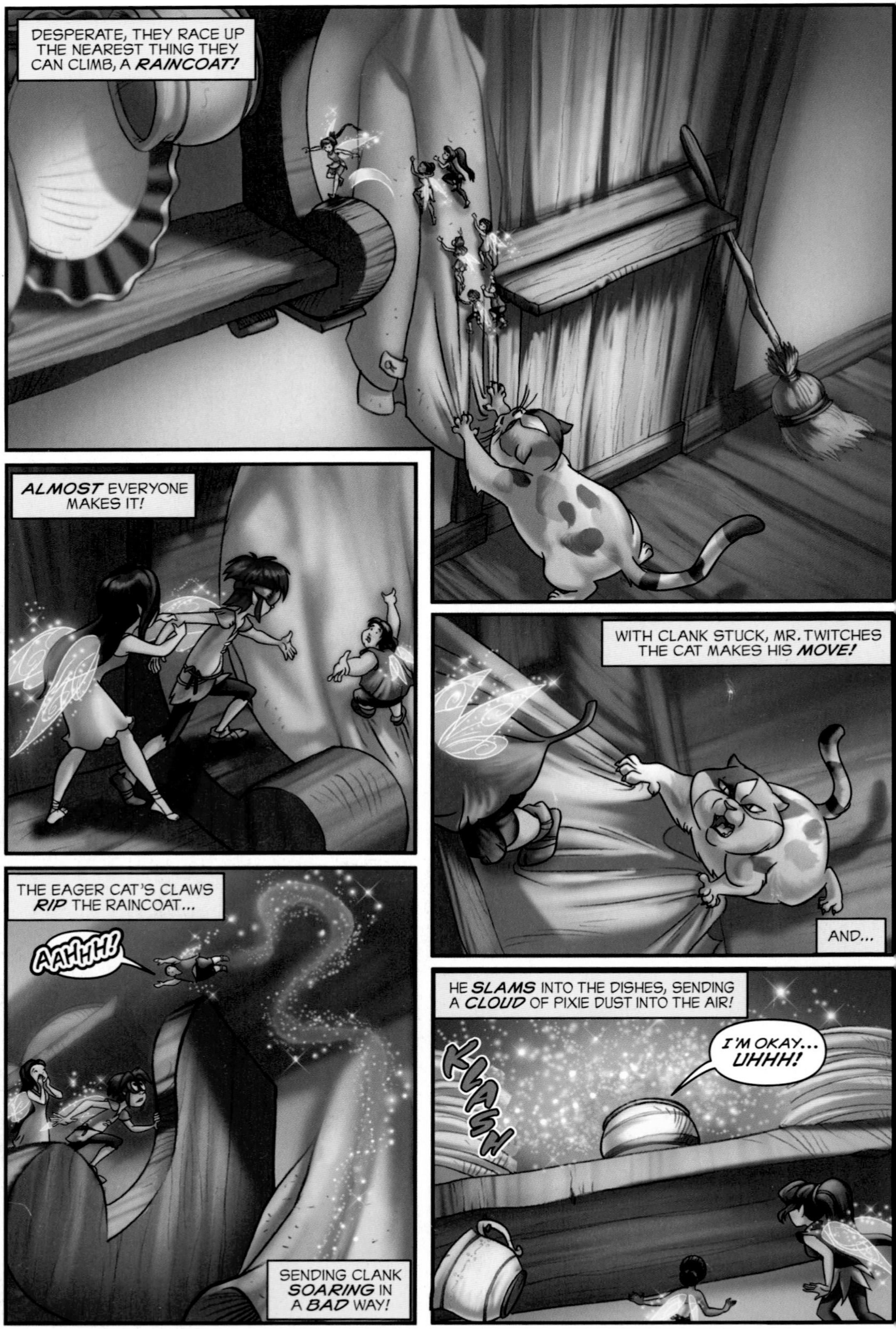
DESPERATE, THEY RACE UP THE NEAREST THING THEY CAN CLIMB, A RAINCOAT!
ALMOST EVERYONE MAKES IT!
WITH CLANK STUCK, MR. TWITCHES THE CAT MAKES HIS MOVE!
AND...
THE EAGER CAT'S CLAWS RIP THE RAINCOAT...
AAHHH!
SENDING CLANK SOARING IN A BAD WAY!
HE SLAMS INTO THE DISHES, SENDING A CLOUD OF PIXIE DUST INTO THE AIR!
KLASH
I'M OKAY... UHHH!

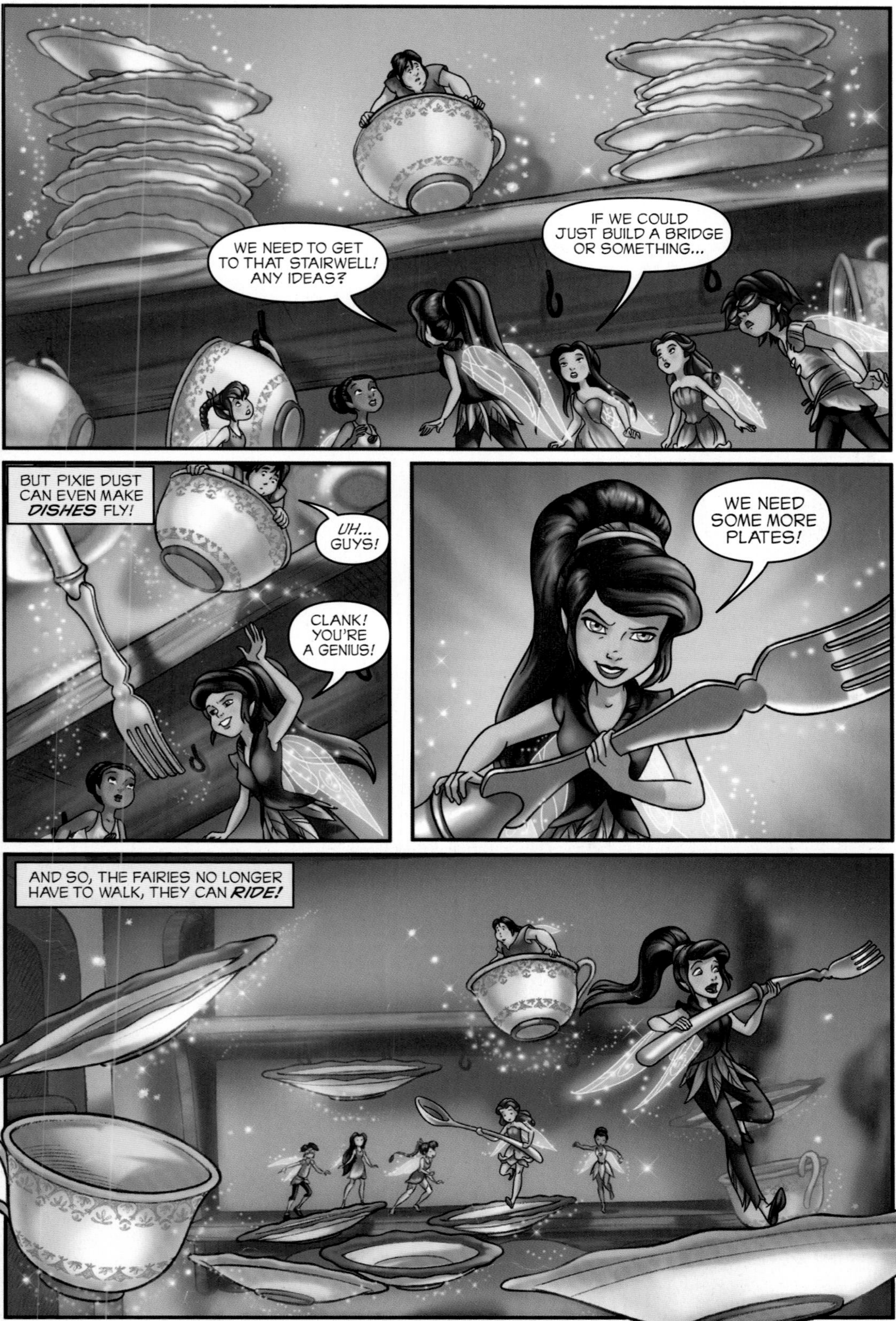
WE NEED TO GET TO THAT STAIRWELL! ANY IDEAS?
IF WE COULD JUST BUILD A BRIDGE OR SOMETHING...
BUT PIXIE DUST CAN EVEN MAKE *DISHES* FLY!
UH... GUYS!
CLANK! YOU'RE A GENIUS!
WE NEED SOME MORE PLATES!
AND SO, THE FAIRIES NO LONGER HAVE TO WALK, THEY CAN *RIDE!*

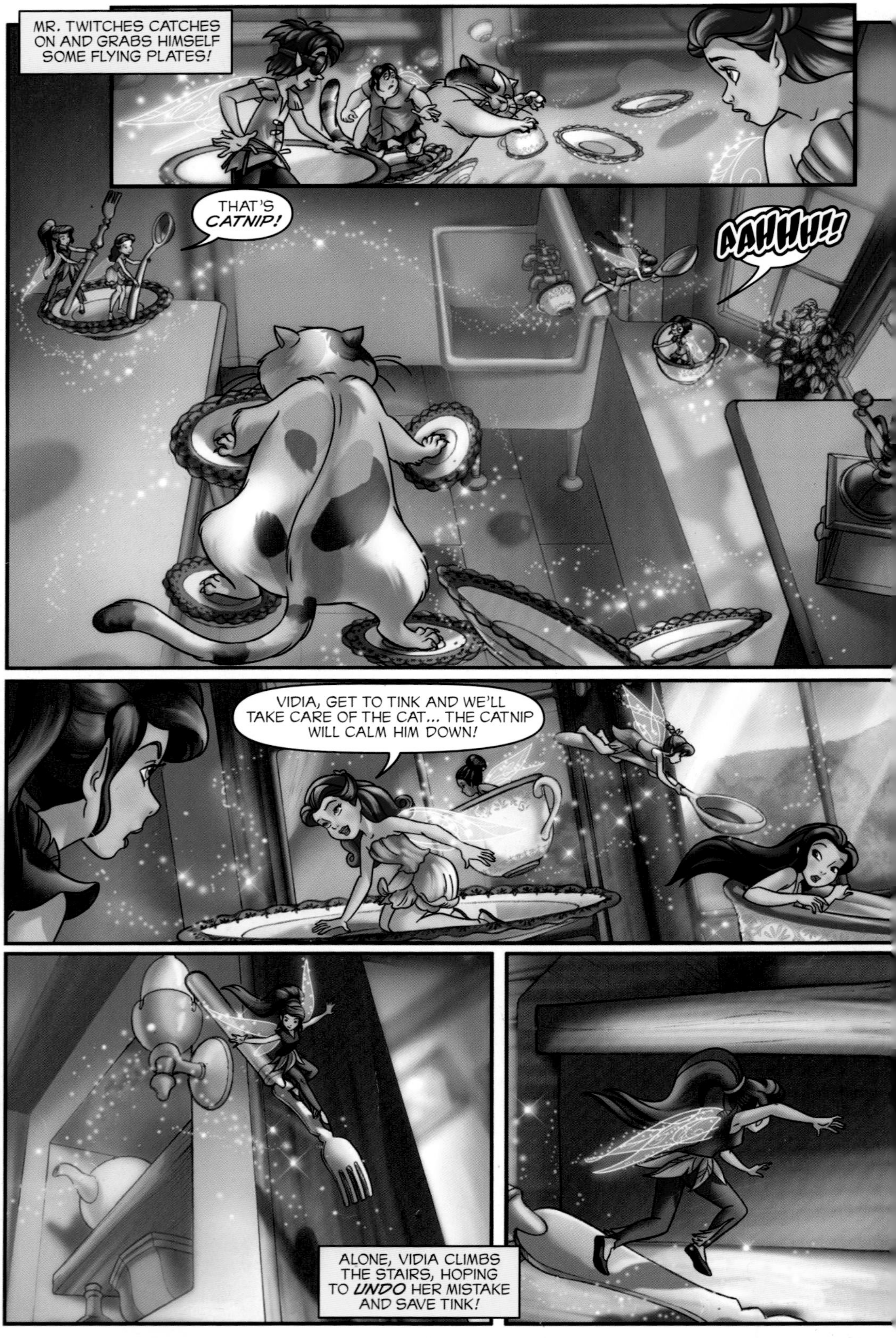
MR. TWITCHES CATCHES ON AND GRABS HIMSELF SOME FLYING PLATES!
THAT'S *CATNIP!*
AAHHH!!
VIDIA, GET TO TINK AND WE'LL TAKE CARE OF THE CAT... THE CATNIP WILL CALM HIM DOWN!
ALONE, VIDIA CLIMBS THE STAIRS, HOPING TO *UNDO* HER MISTAKE AND SAVE TINK!

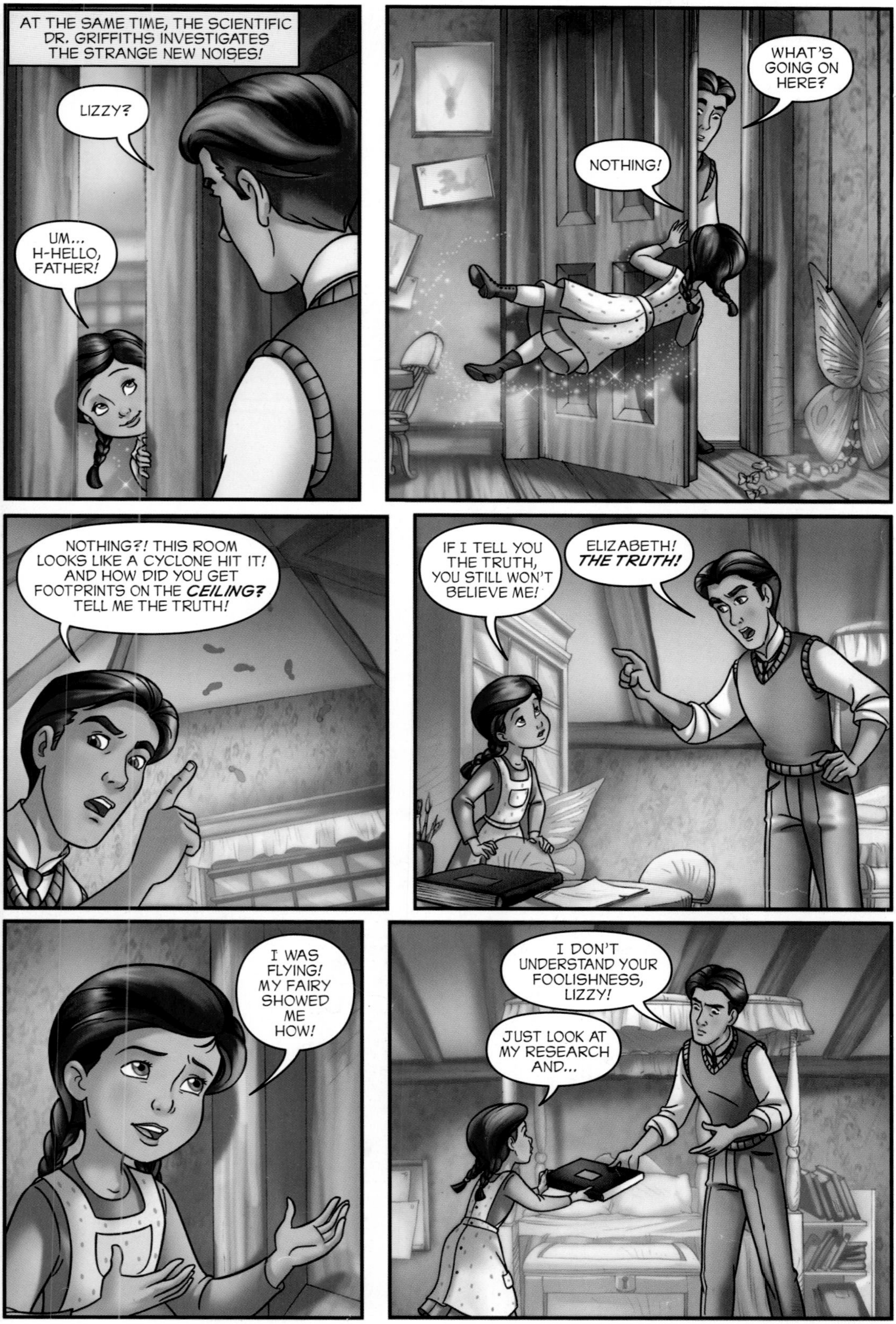
AT THE SAME TIME, THE SCIENTIFIC DR. GRIFFITHS INVESTIGATES THE STRANGE NEW NOISES!
LIZZY?
UM... H-HELLO, FATHER!
WHAT'S GOING ON HERE?
NOTHING!
NOTHING?! THIS ROOM LOOKS LIKE A CYCLONE HIT IT! AND HOW DID YOU GET FOOTPRINTS ON THE CEILING? TELL ME THE TRUTH!
IF I TELL YOU THE TRUTH, YOU STILL WON'T BELIEVE ME!
ELIZABETH! THE TRUTH!
I WAS FLYING! MY FAIRY SHOWED ME HOW!
I DON'T UNDERSTAND YOUR FOOLISHNESS, LIZZY!
JUST LOOK AT MY RESEARCH AND...

I KNOW THIS IS DIFFICULT FOR YOU TO UNDERSTAND, BUT THIS IS ALL *MAKE-BELIEVE!*

NO, THEY'RE REAL!

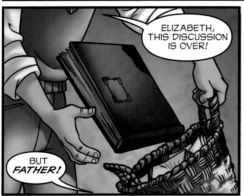

ELIZABETH, THIS DISCUSSION IS OVER!

BUT *FATHER!*

ENOUGH IS ENOUGH, EVEN FOR A FAIRY! TINK CAN *NOT* LET THIS STAND!

EVEN IF IT MEANS *BREAKING* THE RULES AND SHOWING *HERSELF!*

!

SEE! FAIRIES ARE *REAL!*

DING JINGLE DING-A-LING

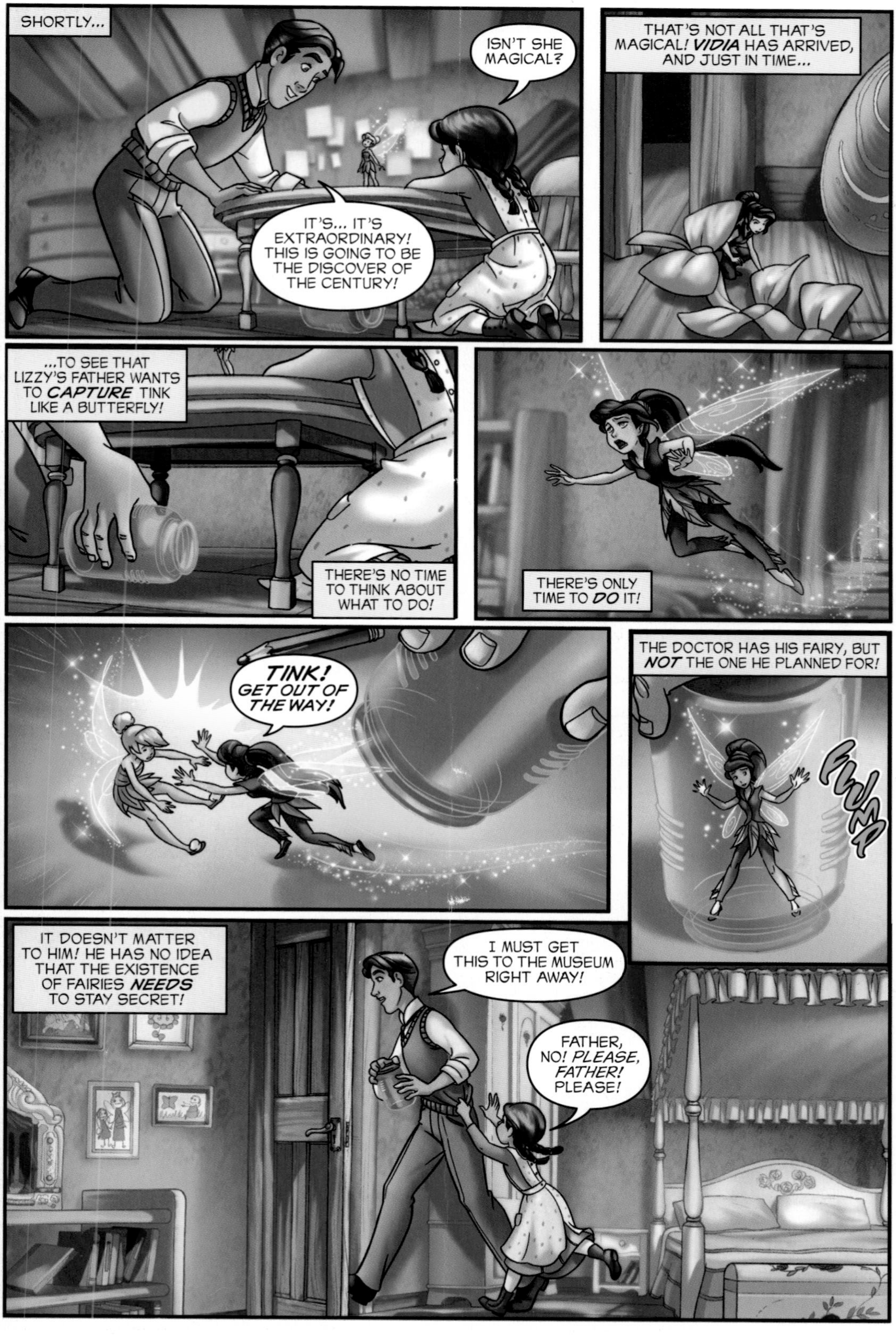
SHORTLY...
ISN'T SHE MAGICAL?
IT'S... IT'S EXTRAORDINARY! THIS IS GOING TO BE THE DISCOVER OF THE CENTURY!
THAT'S NOT ALL THAT'S MAGICAL! VIDIA HAS ARRIVED, AND JUST IN TIME...
...TO SEE THAT LIZZY'S FATHER WANTS TO CAPTURE TINK LIKE A BUTTERFLY!
THERE'S NO TIME TO THINK ABOUT WHAT TO DO!
THERE'S ONLY TIME TO DO IT!
TINK! GET OUT OF THE WAY!
THE DOCTOR HAS HIS FAIRY, BUT NOT THE ONE HE PLANNED FOR!
FWUMP
IT DOESN'T MATTER TO HIM! HE HAS NO IDEA THAT THE EXISTENCE OF FAIRIES NEEDS TO STAY SECRET!
I MUST GET THIS TO THE MUSEUM RIGHT AWAY!
FATHER, NO! PLEASE, FATHER! PLEASE!

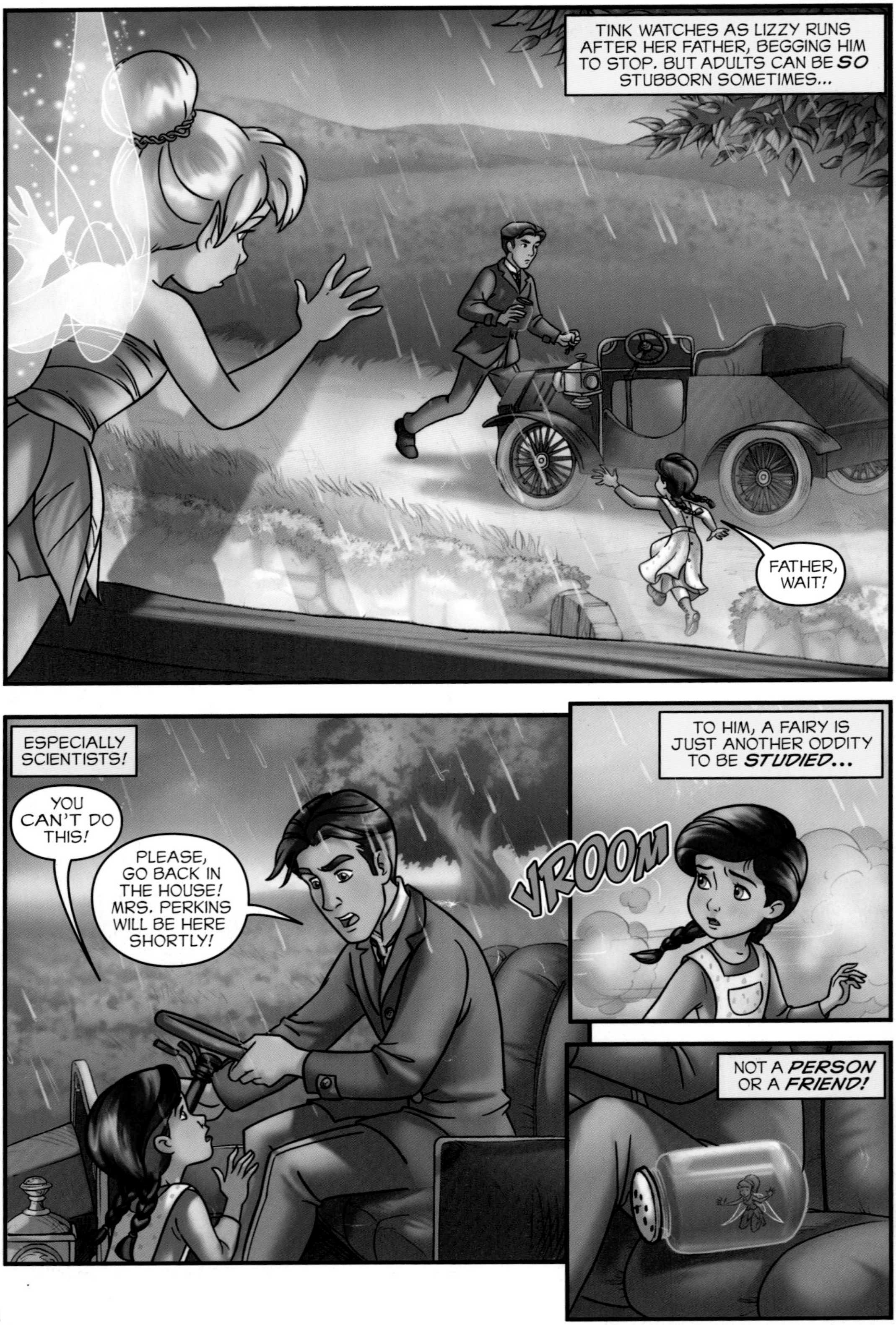

TINK WATCHES AS LIZZY RUNS AFTER HER FATHER, BEGGING HIM TO STOP. BUT ADULTS CAN BE *SO* STUBBORN SOMETIMES...
FATHER, WAIT!
ESPECIALLY SCIENTISTS!
YOU CAN'T DO THIS!
PLEASE, GO BACK IN THE HOUSE! MRS. PERKINS WILL BE HERE SHORTLY!
TO HIM, A FAIRY IS JUST ANOTHER ODDITY TO BE *STUDIED*...
VROOM
NOT A *PERSON* OR A *FRIEND!*

LIZZY HEADS BACK IN, ONLY TO BE DELIGHTED BY ALL THE NEW *COMPANY!*

OH, LOOK! IT'S YOUR FRIENDS!

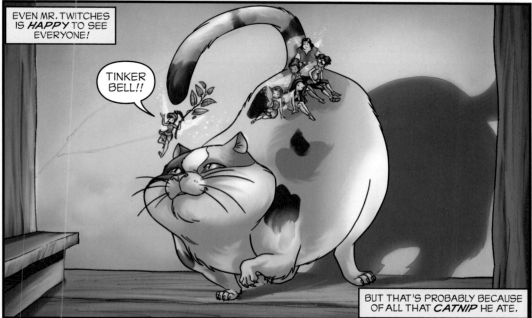

EVEN MR. TWITCHES IS *HAPPY* TO SEE EVERYONE!

TINKER BELL!!

BUT THAT'S PROBABLY BECAUSE OF ALL THAT *CATNIP* HE ATE.

TINKER BELL... ARE YOU OKAY, SWEET PEA?

WHAT HAPPENED?

DING JINGLE DING-A-LING

LIZZY'S FATHER TRAPPED VIDIA IN A JAR!

43

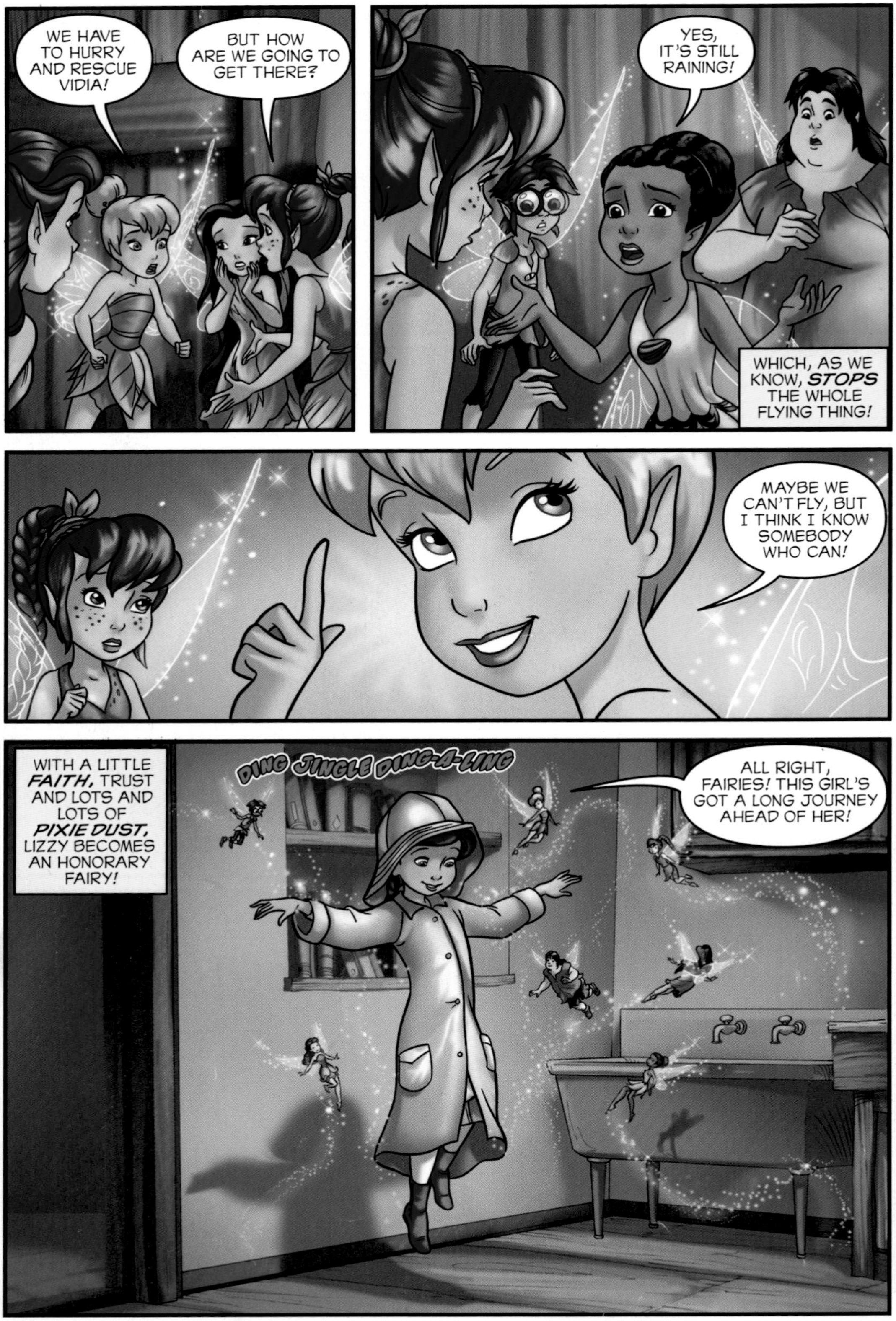
WE HAVE TO HURRY AND RESCUE VIDIA!
BUT HOW ARE WE GOING TO GET THERE?
YES, IT'S STILL RAINING!
WHICH, AS WE KNOW, STOPS THE WHOLE FLYING THING!
MAYBE WE CAN'T FLY, BUT I THINK I KNOW SOMEBODY WHO CAN!
WITH A LITTLE FAITH, TRUST AND LOTS AND LOTS OF PIXIE DUST, LIZZY BECOMES AN HONORARY FAIRY!
DING JINGLE DING-A-LING
ALL RIGHT, FAIRIES! THIS GIRL'S GOT A LONG JOURNEY AHEAD OF HER!

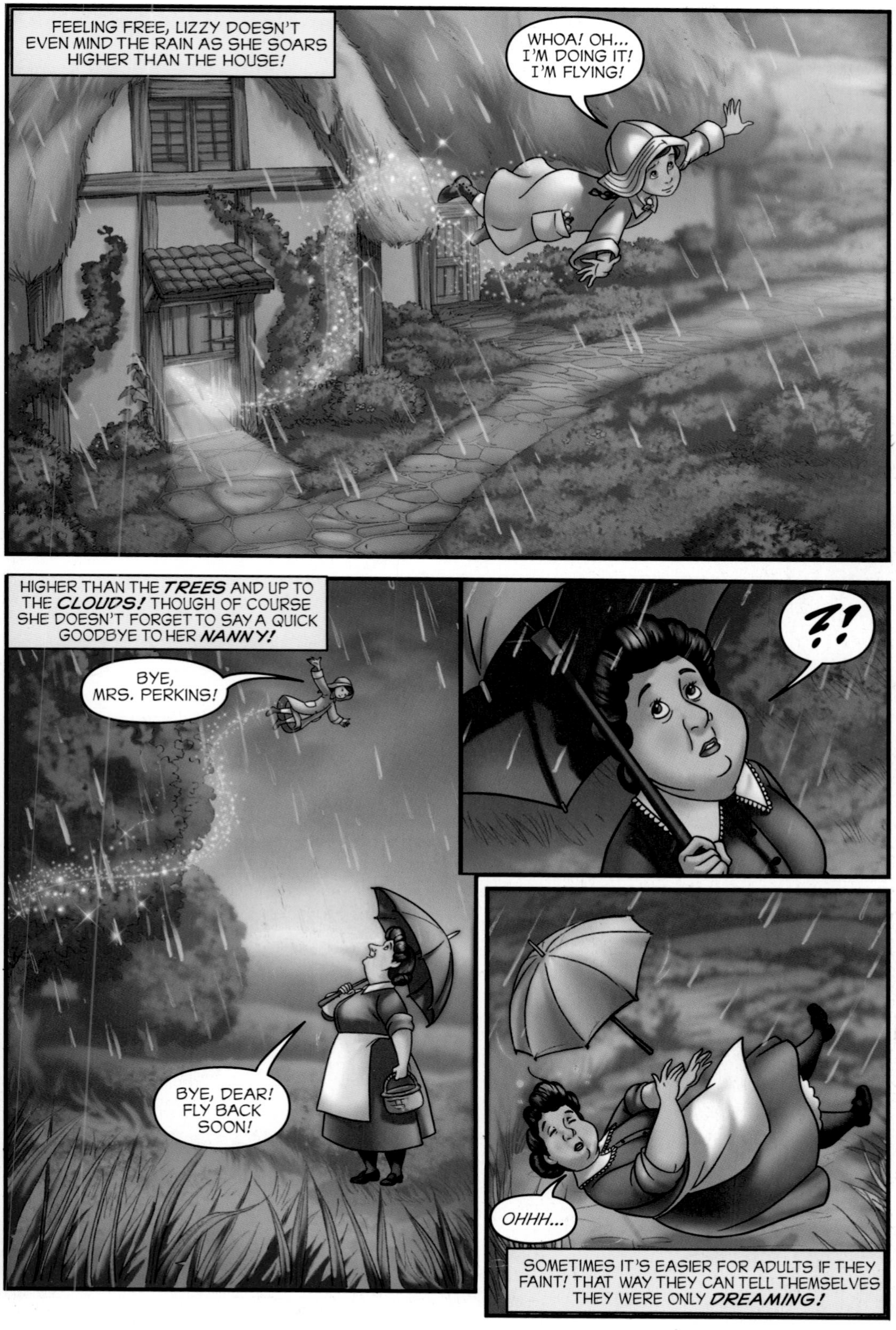
FEELING FREE, LIZZY DOESN'T EVEN MIND THE RAIN AS SHE SOARS HIGHER THAN THE HOUSE!
WHOA! OH... I'M DOING IT! I'M FLYING!
HIGHER THAN THE *TREES* AND UP TO THE *CLOUDS!* THOUGH OF COURSE SHE DOESN'T FORGET TO SAY A QUICK GOODBYE TO HER *NANNY!*
BYE, MRS. PERKINS!
BYE, DEAR! FLY BACK SOON!
?!
OHHH...
SOMETIMES IT'S EASIER FOR ADULTS IF THEY FAINT! THAT WAY THEY CAN TELL THEMSELVES THEY WERE ONLY *DREAMING!*

VIDIA *POUNDS* THE THICK GLASS WITH HER TINY FISTS, TRYING TO ROLL THE JAR OFF THE SEAT AND FREE HERSELF.

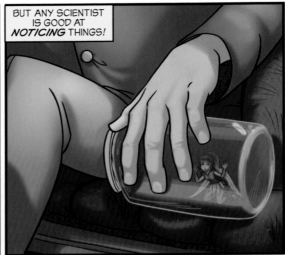

BUT ANY SCIENTIST IS GOOD AT *NOTICING* THINGS!

AND DR. GRIFFITHS ONLY HAS TO KEEP HER *TRAPPED* JUST A LITTLE LONGER!

OR SO HE THINKS! HE HAS *NO* IDEA JUST *WHO* IS FOLLOWING!

TINK, I CAN'T KEEP UP! HE'S *TOO FAST!*

EVEN A *CAR* IS NO MATCH FOR A DETERMINED FAIRY! TINK *DIVES* LIKE SHE'S NEVER DIVED BEFORE!

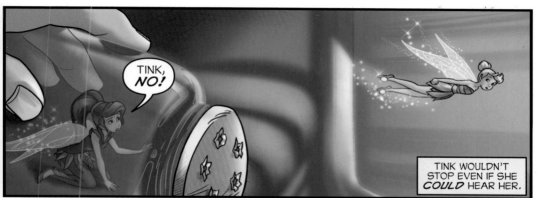

TINK, NO!

TINK WOULDN'T STOP EVEN IF SHE *COULD* HEAR HER.

SHE HEADS RIGHT *UNDER* THE CAR...

AND TAKES A LOOK AT ITS *MYSTERIOUS* MOTOR!

CHUG

CHUG

CHUG

FORTUNATELY, TINKER FAIRIES AREN'T *ONLY* GOOD AT FIXING THINGS!

THEY *ALSO* KNOW HOW TO *BREAK* THEM!

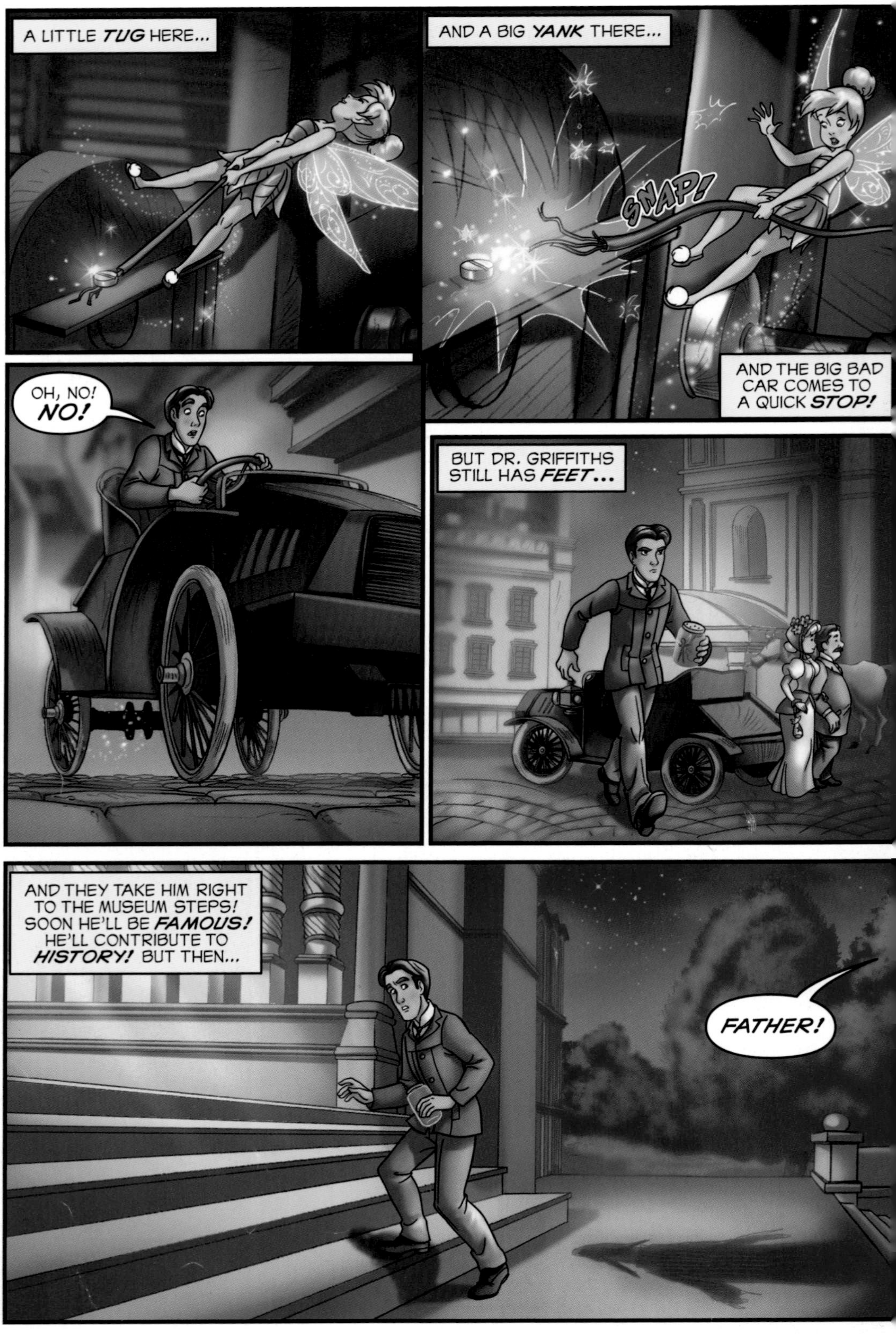
A LITTLE TUG HERE...
AND A BIG YANK THERE...
SNAP!
AND THE BIG BAD CAR COMES TO A QUICK STOP!
OH, NO! NO!
BUT DR. GRIFFITHS STILL HAS FEET...
AND THEY TAKE HIM RIGHT TO THE MUSEUM STEPS! SOON HE'LL BE FAMOUS! HE'LL CONTRIBUTE TO HISTORY! BUT THEN...
FATHER!

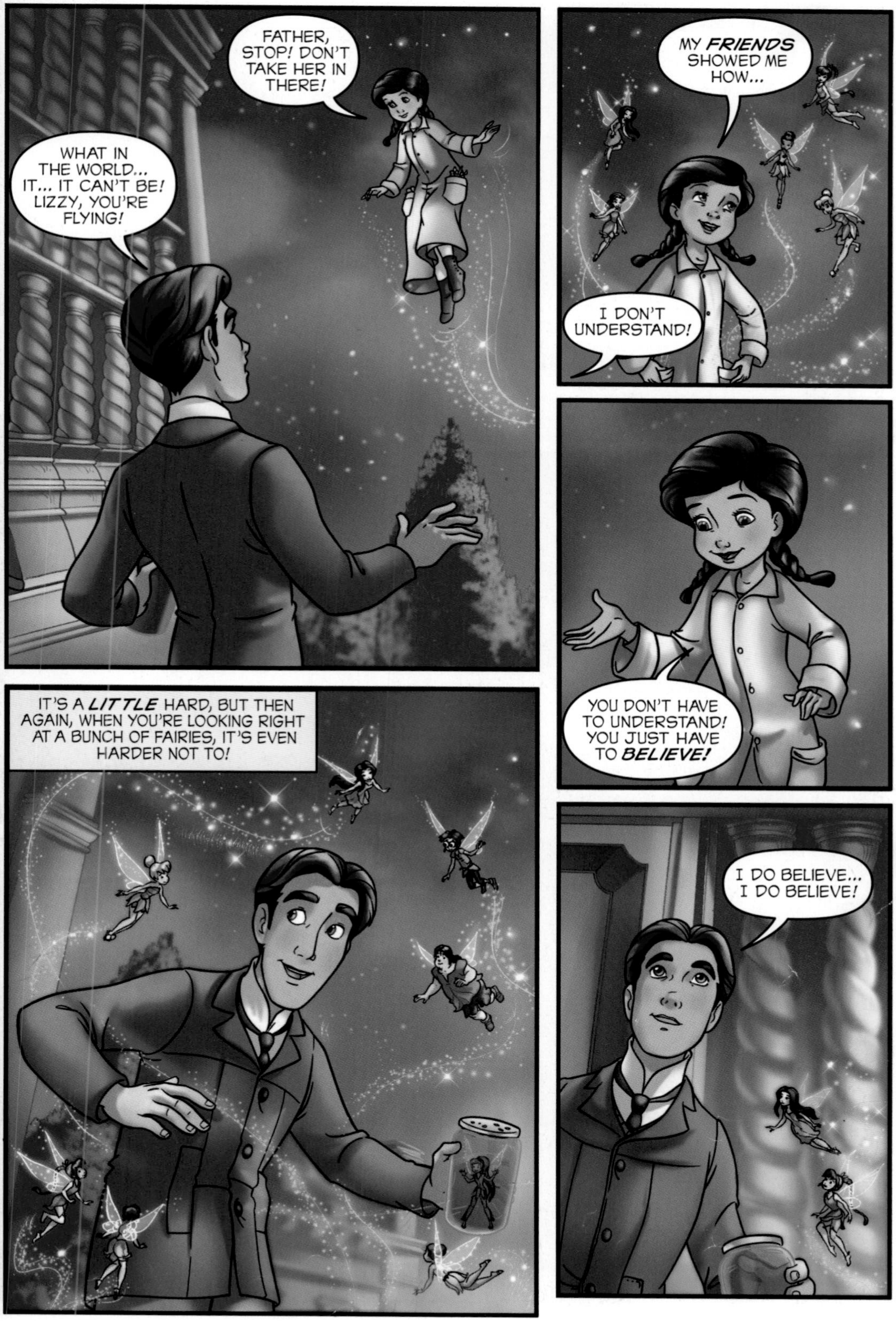
FATHER, STOP! DON'T TAKE HER IN THERE!
WHAT IN THE WORLD... IT... IT CAN'T BE! LIZZY, YOU'RE FLYING!
MY FRIENDS SHOWED ME HOW...
I DON'T UNDERSTAND!
YOU DON'T HAVE TO UNDERSTAND! YOU JUST HAVE TO BELIEVE!
IT'S A LITTLE HARD, BUT THEN AGAIN, WHEN YOU'RE LOOKING RIGHT AT A BUNCH OF FAIRIES, IT'S EVEN HARDER NOT TO!
I DO BELIEVE... I DO BELIEVE!

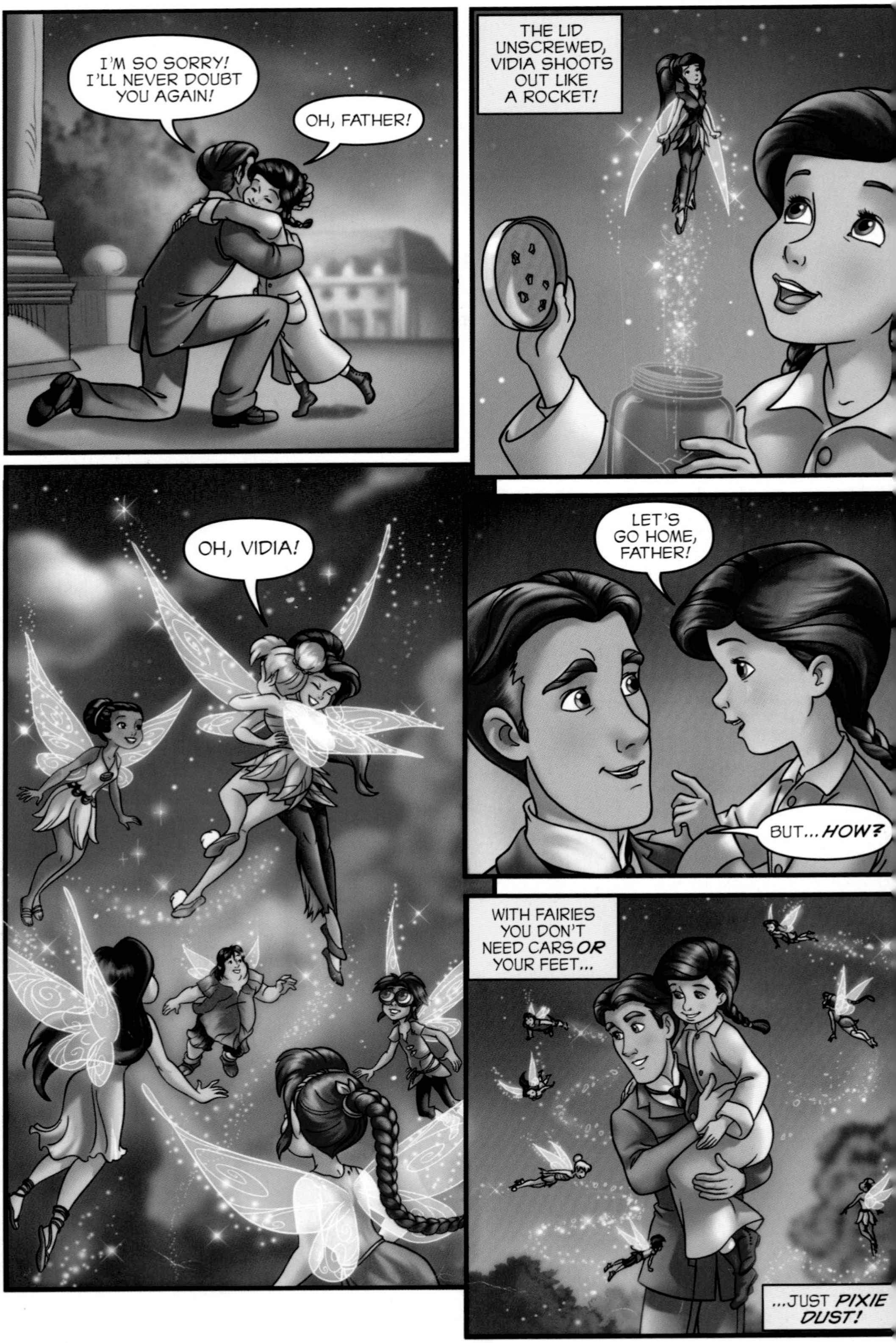
I'M SO SORRY! I'LL NEVER DOUBT YOU AGAIN!
OH, FATHER!
THE LID UNSCREWED, VIDIA SHOOTS OUT LIKE A ROCKET!
OH, VIDIA!
LET'S GO HOME, FATHER!
BUT... HOW?
WITH FAIRIES YOU DON'T NEED CARS OR YOUR FEET...
...JUST PIXIE DUST!

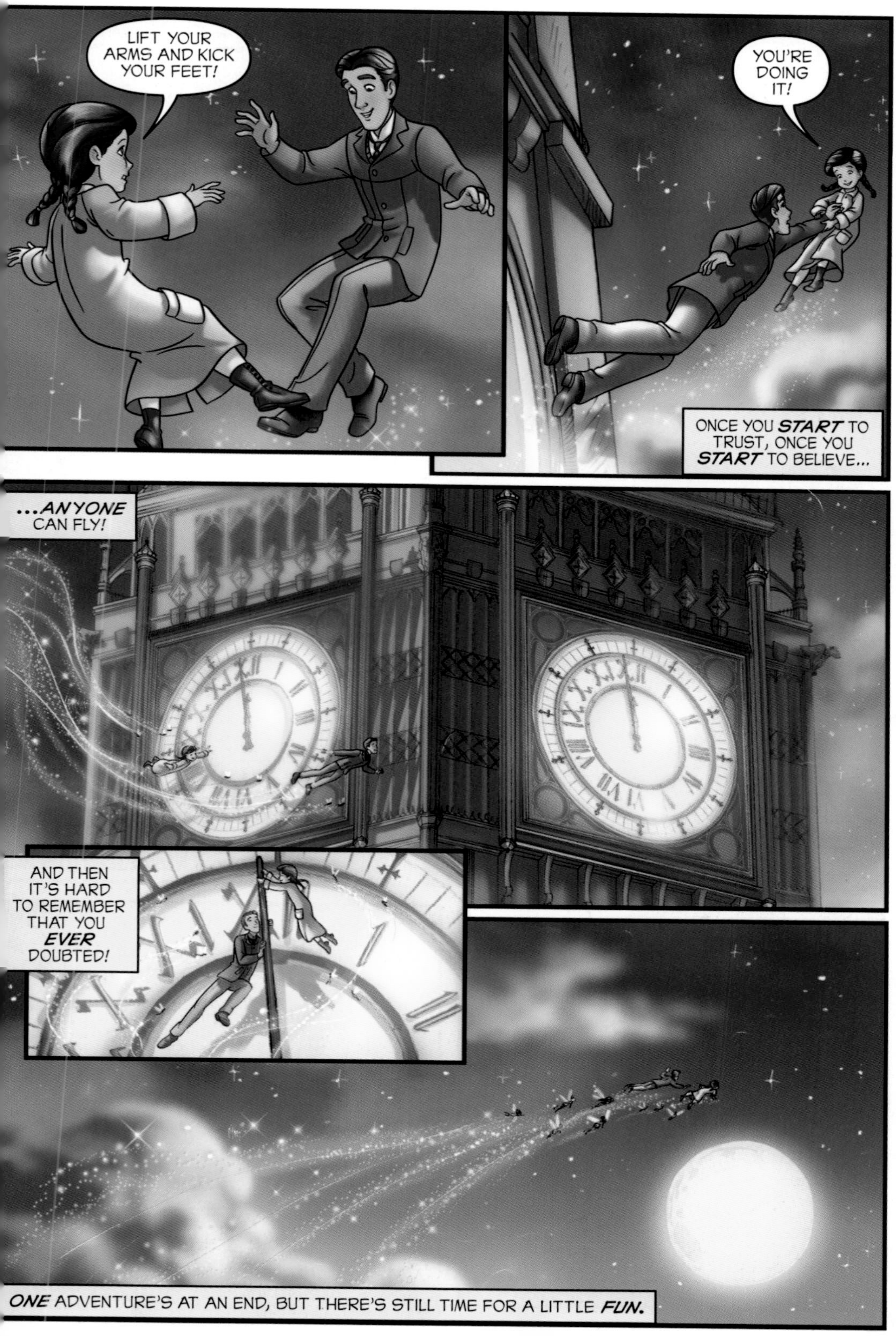
LIFT YOUR ARMS AND KICK YOUR FEET!
YOU'RE DOING IT!
ONCE YOU START TO TRUST, ONCE YOU START TO BELIEVE...
...ANYONE CAN FLY!
AND THEN IT'S HARD TO REMEMBER THAT YOU EVER DOUBTED!
ONE ADVENTURE'S AT AN END, BUT THERE'S STILL TIME FOR A LITTLE FUN.

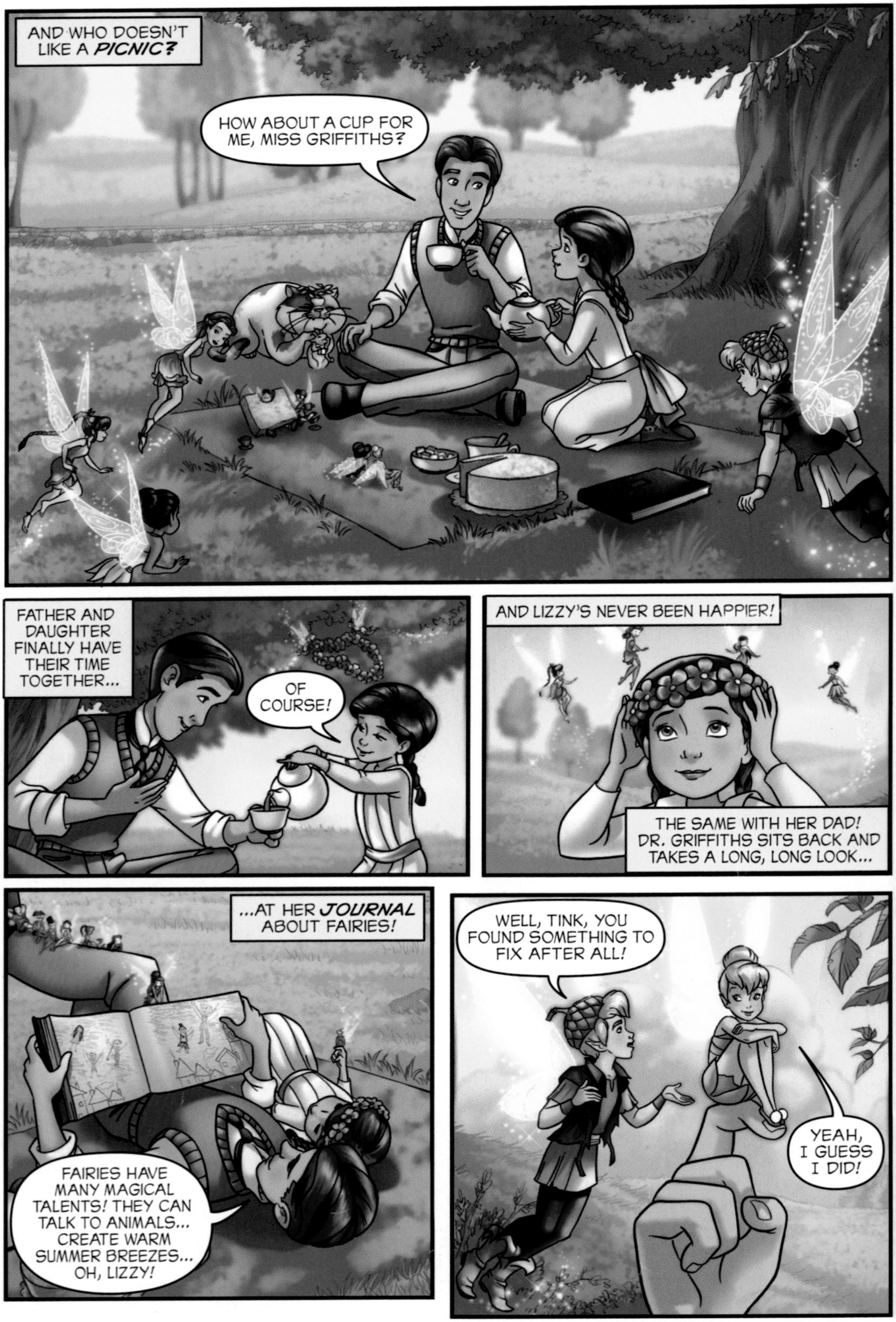
AND WHO DOESN'T LIKE A PICNIC?
HOW ABOUT A CUP FOR ME, MISS GRIFFITHS?
FATHER AND DAUGHTER FINALLY HAVE THEIR TIME TOGETHER...
OF COURSE!
AND LIZZY'S NEVER BEEN HAPPIER!
THE SAME WITH HER DAD! DR. GRIFFITHS SITS BACK AND TAKES A LONG, LONG LOOK...
...AT HER JOURNAL ABOUT FAIRIES!
FAIRIES HAVE MANY MAGICAL TALENTS! THEY CAN TALK TO ANIMALS... CREATE WARM SUMMER BREEZES... OH, LIZZY!
WELL, TINK, YOU FOUND SOMETHING TO FIX AFTER ALL!
YEAH, I GUESS I DID!

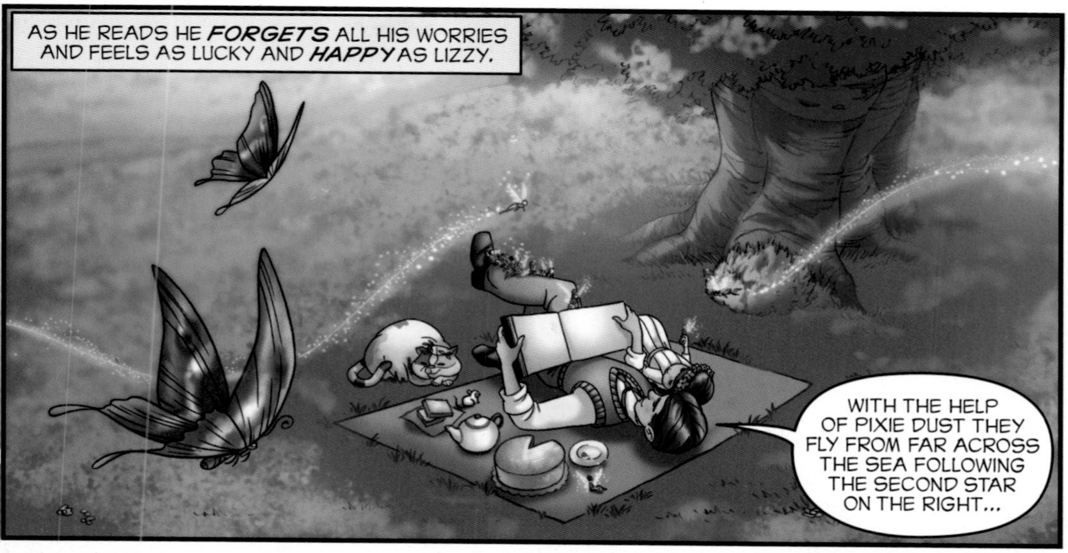
AS HE READS HE FORGETS ALL HIS WORRIES AND FEELS AS LUCKY AND HAPPY AS LIZZY.
WITH THE HELP OF PIXIE DUST THEY FLY FROM FAR ACROSS THE SEA FOLLOWING THE SECOND STAR ON THE RIGHT...

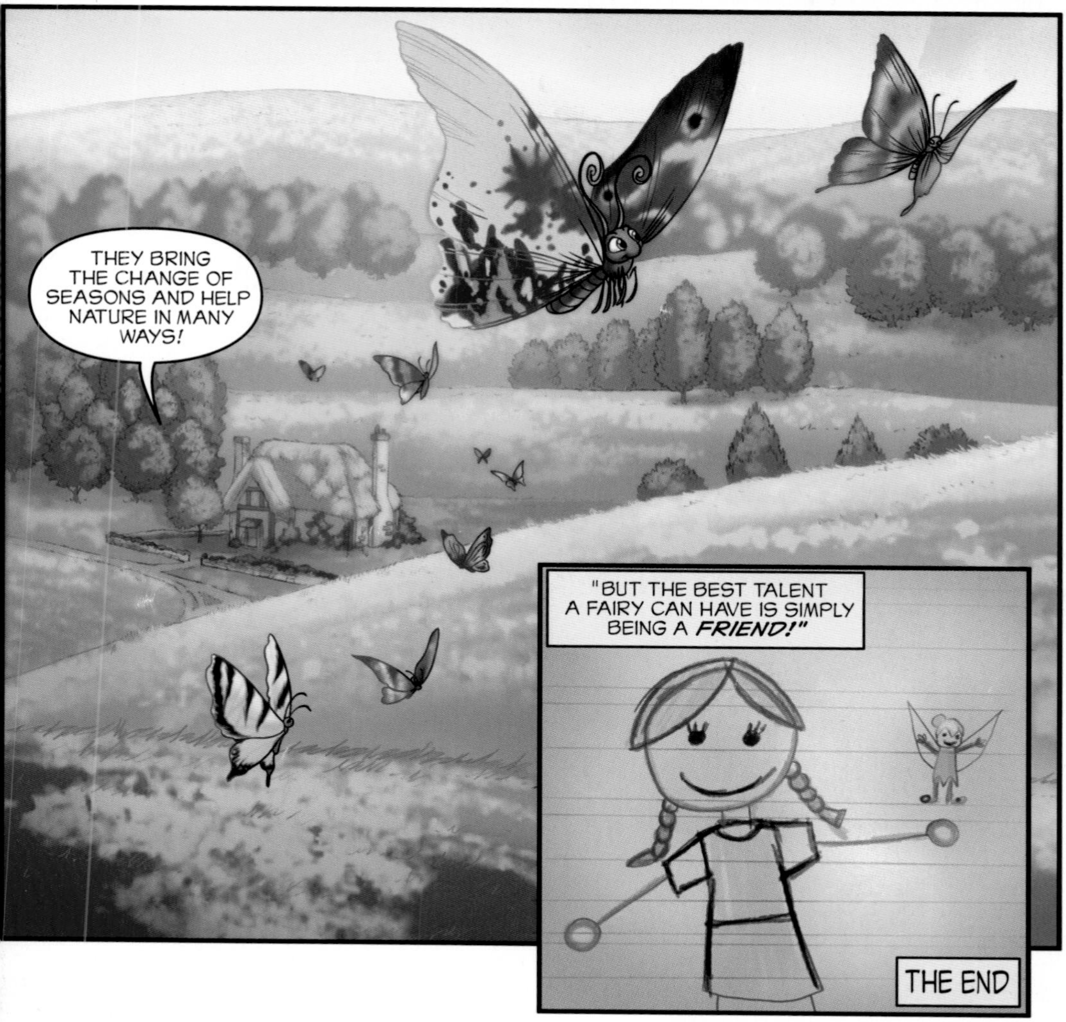
THEY BRING THE CHANGE OF SEASONS AND HELP NATURE IN MANY WAYS!
"BUT THE BEST TALENT A FAIRY CAN HAVE IS SIMPLY BEING A FRIEND!"
THE END

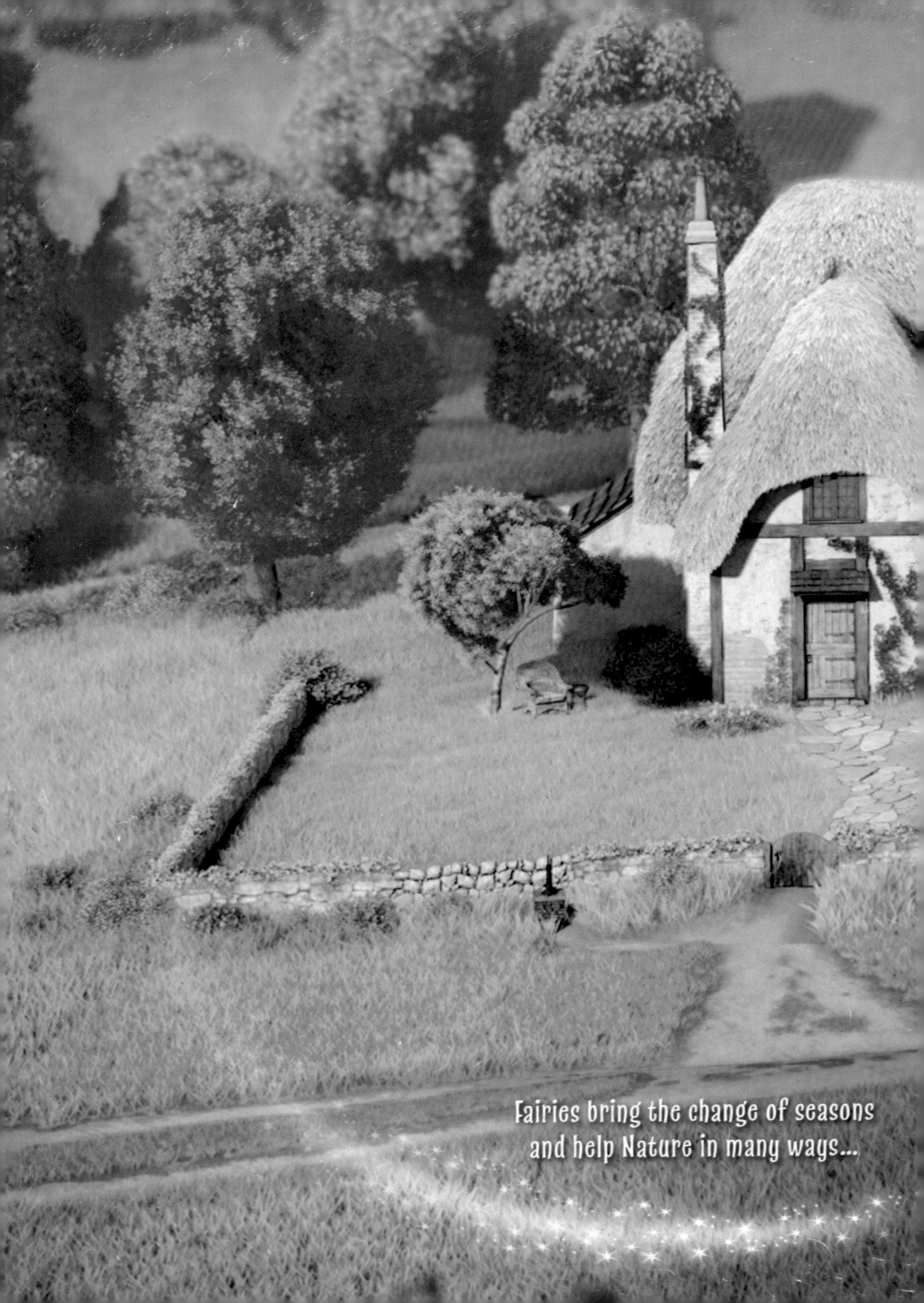

Fairies bring the change of seasons
and help Nature in many ways...

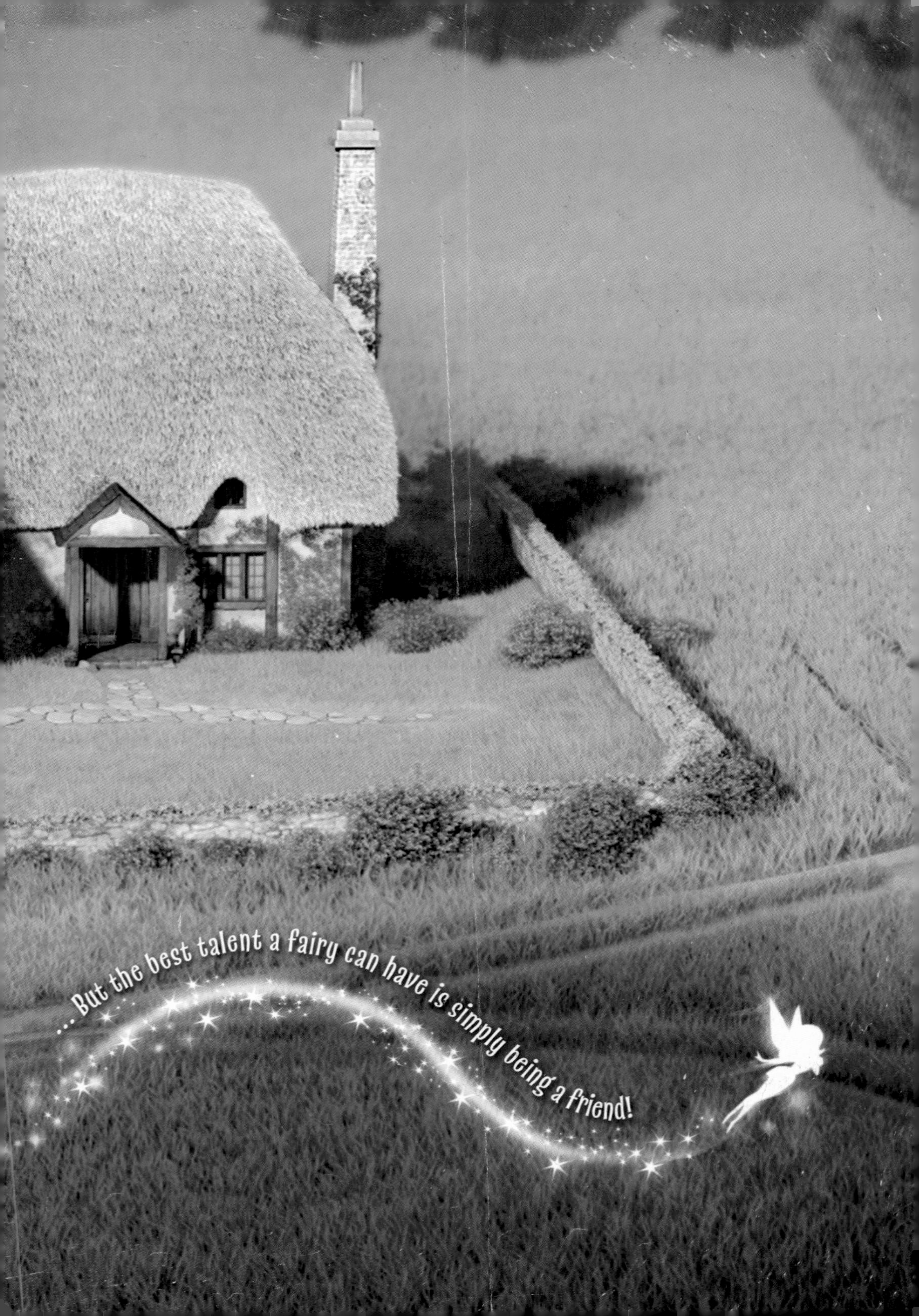

. . . But the best talent a fairy can have is simply being a friend!

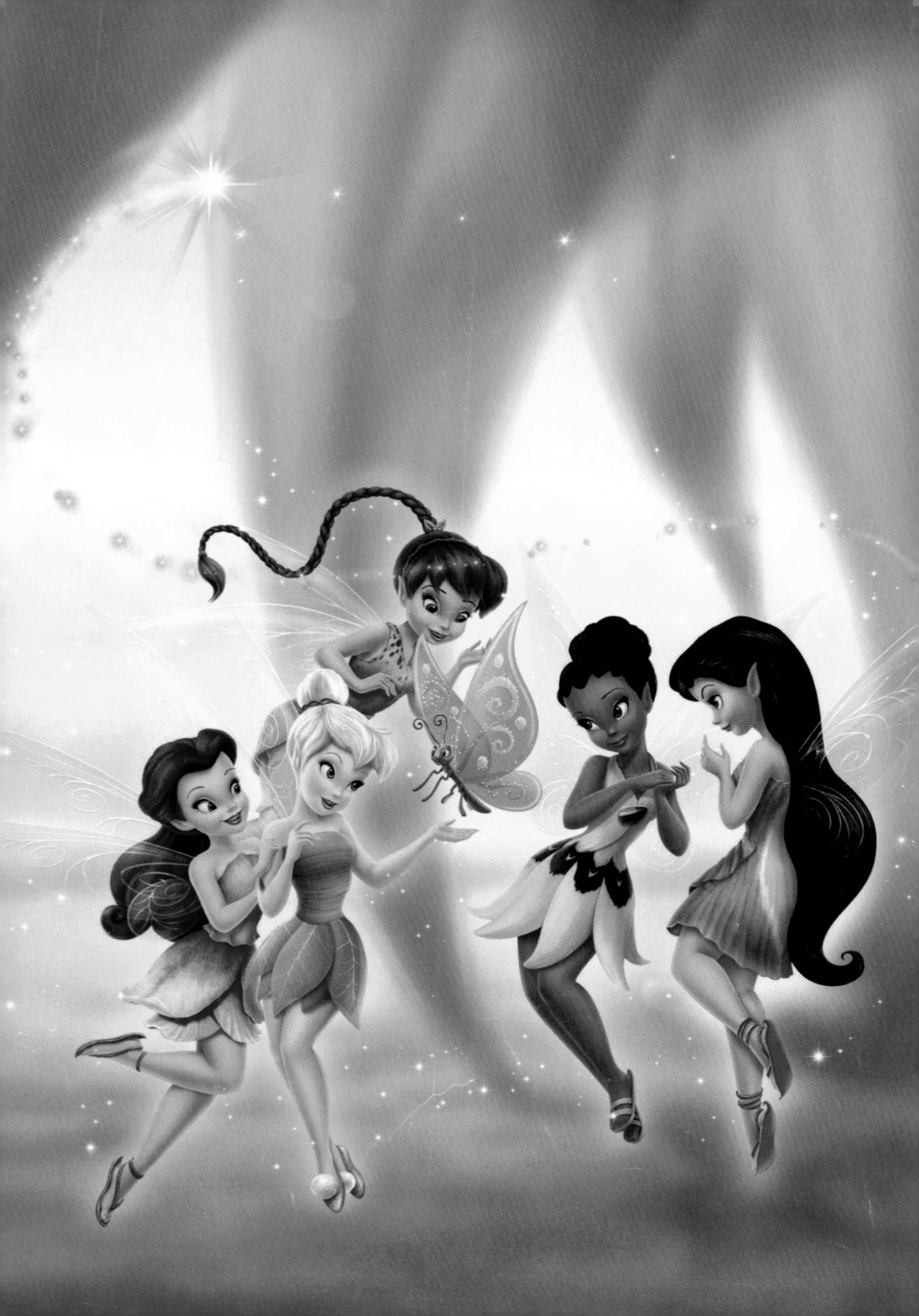

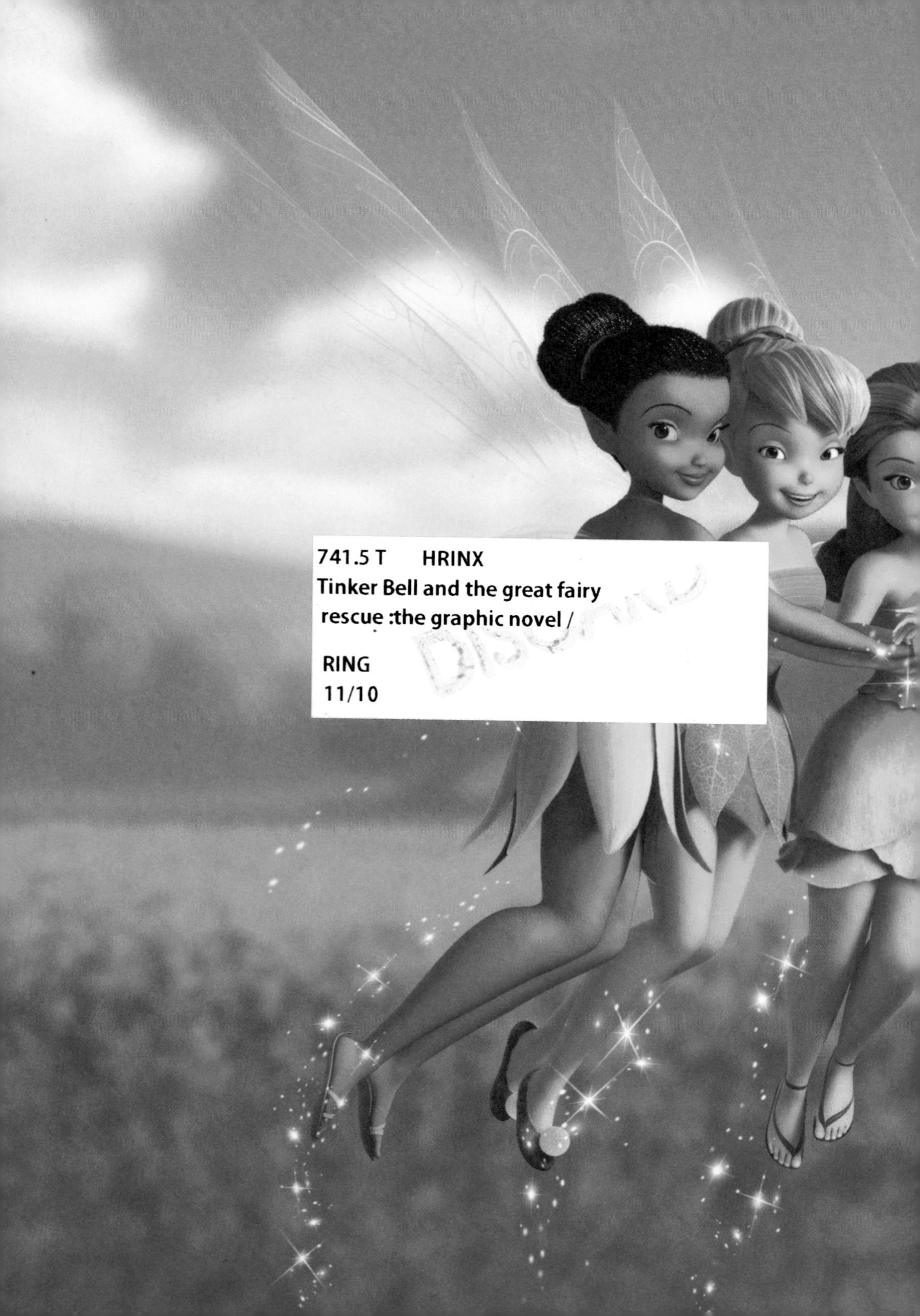